SECOND CHANCES

Wild Justice, Book 1

By Debra Shelton

Published by Sonlight Publishing Ltd.

Cover Design by Sonlight Publishing

ISBN-13: 978-1-7327892-2-7
ISBN-10: 1-7327892-3-4

ACKNOWLEDGEMENTS

I'd like to offer a special thanks to Kathy McKinsey for her help in editing and for her invaluable feedback.

DEDICATION

To my dad, who filled my life with stories of the Old West. Having actually spent summers in the very cabin Butch and Sundance used in Brown's Park conjured up all kinds of imagined adventures and set my mind to dancing.

CHAPTER 1

The carrion birds swung in a lazy circle high above the parched, desolate landscape. Disgruntled and exhausted, Chloe collapsed on the nearest large boulder. She had thousands to choose from across the harsh, unforgiving landscape of Irish Canyon.

Never in her wildest dreams did she imagine herself running for her life in the high desert country of northern Colorado. She listened for the sound of the big cat.

Nothing. Only the wind whistling through the cedars and along the red cliffs. Maybe he had grown tired of chasing her.

I can only hope. Still, she kept her ears tuned for any unusual sound.

She gave a small snort at the thought. She wouldn't know an unusual sound in this godforsaken country, even if it echoed a warning against the steep canyon walls that surrounded her.

"If only Papa and Auntie Clare could see me now."

She stooped to rub the ache out of her leather-clad feet. The heeled boots were stylish, but not very practical for traipsing around in the wilderness. Jasper had tried to talk her into letting him knock the heels off. Now she wished she had listened to him.

Chloe pushed back long, wayward strands of ebony hair and exhaled a puff of air toward the fringe of damp curls on her forehead. She straightened to search the deep pockets of her calico skirt for her hanky. Finding the dainty square of lacy-edged linen, she mopped the sheen of sweat from her brow and the back of her neck.

"What good is being ladylike and fashionable when nobody can see me but a bunch of buzzards and jack rabbits? I hate this place," she grumbled to nobody in particular.

She was a city girl. Born and bred in the bustling metropolis of Philadelphia. Her father, Oliver Cantrell, made sure theirs was one of the first houses to have the latest conveniences. Things like the new electric lights Mr. Edison had invented, indoor plumbing, and a private telephone. Chloe loved to stand across the garden at night and look back at the brightly lit windows or take long, luxurious baths in her own private bathroom. Growing up with these privileges, Chloe accepted them as an ordinary everyday part of life.

Here, smelly kerosene lit Jasper Johnson's tiny cabin and an even smellier outhouse a good forty paces passed a stand of sagebrush. Water had to be pumped, hauled, and heated. An arduous task that curbed Chloe's habit of bathing several times a week.

She wiggled her nose at the smell emanating from the now damp handkerchief. *What I wouldn't give for a long, hot soak in a tub sprinkled with lilac bath salts.*

Chloe frowned and pulled what Auntie Clare called her 'pouty face'. This was nothing like she expected when she answered the newspaper advertisement about a man needing a housekeeper and cook in rural northwestern Colorado.

"Housekeeper indeed." She snorted.

Had she known, she might have changed her mind regardless that this was where she hoped to find her half-brother, Harry. He was the brother she never knew she had until the reading of Papa's will a short four months ago.

It was a shock to think that Papa had an affair with some woman named Anna, let alone finding out he had a son by her. Chloe didn't know the whole story, and now she never would.

The mix of loss and anger that wrenched at her heart hadn't eased with her journey west. She vowed not to judge the man she loved and admired above all others.

If her calculations were correct, this mystery offspring would be ten years older than her, making him thirty-two. Did he have her father's features or stand as tall as the man she adored? Would he acknowledge her as his sister once he found out the truth of his birth? A million questions had plagued Chloe's mind since Mr. Stanley had read the particulars to her regarding her inheritance.

It seemed she could not receive the bulk of her father's estate until she located this Harry Longabaugh and convinced him to come back to Pennsylvania with her. Cantrell Firearms needed a man to run it. And apparently, Papa thought Harry fit the bill better than she did.

She gave another displeased snort at the thought that her own father had so little faith in her abilities. When her mother died of influenza and left three-year-old Chloe in the care of her father, Chloe became a fixture around the arms factory. She knew every nook and cranny of the huge old building and was the pet of many of the workers.

By the time she was a teenager, she could name every part to a half dozen different types of guns. She knew every one of her father's suppliers and could tell when one was trying to cheat them. Even Lucius Wheeler, Papa's plant manager, grudgingly admired Chloe's abilities when it came to guns and business.

A deep sigh dragged her shoulders down and brought a

frown to her face at the thought of Lucius. Not long before her father's death, the man began pestering her with his attention. He'd gone so far as to suggest a courtship might be good for both of them after Mr. Stanley announced the terms of her father's will.

The tumble of stones and a low nicker brought her back to the present. She slid off the rock and crouched behind it. Her first thought—Indians! This was the Wild West, after all. Were there still Indians roaming the countryside in 1899? Jasper's assurance that the few who had escaped being forced onto the reservations were harmless, did little to calm her fears.

She ventured a peek. Her eyes scanned the rough path she had come down and continued toward the shadows that dimpled the cliff walls. She brought a hand up to shield her eyes as they traveled up the red rock spires. Like knobby, arthritic fingers, they seemed to reach toward the azure blue of the sky. Shallows flittered in and out of their cone-shaped mud homes in the cliff's crevices.

Something moved on the rim. Chloe gasped and fell back against the rough stone. A man on a horse! Had he seen her? Was it a real Indian or maybe an outlaw? Jasper said gangs of outlaws regularly holed up in the area to avoid the law.

She estimated he was only thirty feet above her. She was trapped. From his vantage point, he would surely see her the minute she moved from behind the rock. She shivered against its heat. *Don't panic. Papa would tell me to think through my options.*

Where was the sun? She looked up at the sky. Definitely well to the west. Surely, Jasper would come looking for her when he came back and realized she hadn't fixed his supper. The problem was, he wouldn't know about the huge golden cat spooking her into running pall mall down this little used animal trail.

It wasn't until last week that she would even consider venturing beyond the little creek that ran along the base of the hillside where Jasper's cabin squatted. After a run-in with a snake longer than she was tall, Chloe refused to go past the spring. It took the old man days to convince her that the bull snake he called Brutus was harmless.

~

"I can still see you, you know."

Trace Rawlings swung a leg over and eased himself down off the roan. It felt good to get out of the saddle. He arched his back to relieve his tired muscles.

The girl didn't move. At least not the hem of her blue dress or the tip of her boot. That was all he could see of her as she ducked back behind the large boulder she'd been sitting on when he rode up on the rim above her.

He squatted down and picked up a couple of marble-sized pebbles. A calculated smirk worked his mouth as he aimed and shot the first one. It pinged off the rock just above where her head should be. The foot moved out of sight.

"What's a little girl like you doing out here traipsing around all alone, anyway?"

Without stepping into view, a young, feminine voice replied. "For your information I'm NOT a little girl and who says I'm alone?"

Trace's trained eye skimmed over the landscape and stiffened. She was right, she wasn't alone. He stood and eased his sidearm from the holster that hung from his right hip. In one smooth motion, he sighted the gun and drew the hammer back. He would have preferred the Winchester for the distance, but the rifle scabbard hung from the other side of his saddle. The shot rang out and echoed off the surrounding canyon walls. In the same instant, the girl screamed.

CHAPTER 2

Chloe curled into a tight ball at the base of the rock, her hands over her ears, and her eyes squeezed shut. *He's trying to shoot me! Oh, Lord, now what am I going to do?*

The thought was more than a statement. She learned to have conversations with God as a little girl growing up. Her Auntie Clare talked to God all day as if he was standing in the same room with her and answering right back. Now she wished she was back in Clare's kitchen helping roll out dough with the big, black woman she thought of as family.

A second shot rang out.

"Please, stop. I'm coming out. Just don't shoot me."

Chloe maneuvered herself around to face the rough surface of the rock. With trembling hands and legs that threatened to give out under her, she began the slow process of pulling herself up to her full five-foot height.

She took a deep, fortifying breath and stepped away from the protection of the boulder. She raised one hand over her head in surrender. The other came down to shield her eyes as she squinted up at the dark figure above her. He moved down the steep slope leading the horse. Loose shale, and the thousand-pound animal behind him, made him cautious. The long barrel of the gun pointed in her direction. Would he shoot a defenseless woman?

"Please, I'm unarmed. My husband will be looking for me," she lied. "I need to get home."

The silhouette changed from a dark shape to a full-color image of a man as he came to a stop a few feet away. It surprised her to see he was young, no more than twenty-eight or twenty-nine. His lean form stood a head and a half taller than her. Tanned, rugged features, and several days' growth of beard emphasized the chiseled line of his jaw. The shadow of his hat partially hid his eyes. The combination gave him a dangerous look.

He holstered the pistol as he walked up. With a finger he pushed back his black Stetson Boss to reveal a sweaty lock of dark, auburn hair. A startled expression flashed in his icy blue eyes for a second.

"What's a young lady like you doing out here, alone and unprotected?"

"May I?" Chloe raised her eyes to her extended arm.

"Sure. I didn't ask you to put your hands up. It's not like I'm the sheriff and you're under arrest." He crossed his arms. Chloe stared as muscle strained against the plaid fabric.

Tearing her eyes away, she looked back up into the menacing-looking face. He quirked an eyebrow. One corner of his mouth rose with it giving him an intimidating scowl.

Determined not to show fear, she dropped her arms to her sides and turned to head back along the path. "I'll just be going now. I need to get my husband's supper cooking."

"Hold up a minute there, ma'am." He reached out and grabbed her arm.

Chloe looked back at where his fingers burned a circling band of heat through the flowered sleeve and into her skin. "Please, take your hands off me," she stammered. She lifted her chin and tried with all her might to look haughty and in control.

He instantly released her and raised his own hands in mock surrender. "Sorry, lady. I'm just trying to save your pretty little hide, but if you know better—than sure, go ahead—leave." He turned and swung effortlessly back into the saddle. The horse groaned and shied toward her, causing her to step back and almost stumble.

Chloe steadied herself. "I'll be going now. Back to my husband."

The man rested his arms across the saddle horn and leaned forward. "Okay."

She turned, sucked in a deep breath, and began moving down the narrow track, glad the folds of her dress hid her trembling hands. *Now if I can just manage not to stumble while he's looking.*

"You might want to keep an eye out for that mountain lion that's been stalking you. Pumas aren't known to give up on an easy kill. Those shots were meant to spook him, but I'm sure he didn't go far." Chloe heard him turn his horse and head in the opposite direction. "Good luck, ma'am."

She froze. The big cat was still close? He hadn't been shooting at her? She turned and shouted, "Wait! I thought… I mean I didn't realize he was still tracking me."

As much as she hated to ask, Chloe knew she needed the cowboy's help, outlaw or not. "Could you maybe take me back to the cabin? I got a little turned around, but I think it's only a few miles back in that direction." She pointed down the faint trail she'd come up on.

He pulled in on the reins and turned in the saddle. "Say please."

"What?"

"Figured a lady like you had manners. Guess I was wrong." He clicked his tongue, and the horse moved forward.

Chloe huffed and crossed her arms. Why was he being so obstinate? "Pleeease, sir. Could you offer me a ride back to my home?"

~

Trace grinned and chuckled to himself as he swung the horse around. The girl stood stiff-backed, her arms folded. She thrust her tiny chin out and her rose-tinted lips smoothed to a firm line, losing all the fullness he'd noticed before.

She wasn't a classic beauty like Ann or Josie Bassett, but the promise was there waiting to mature. Something about the chocolate eyes framed in long dark lashes, and the pert little nose, drew him in and teased his senses.

Most of her jet-black tangle of curls had worked loose from the bun that now rode a little off-center on the top of her head. Even with the topknot, she stood a full head and a half shorter than him. It was hard to judge her age, given her stature. He guessed she was in her late teens, maybe twenty.

He pulled the big roan up beside her. Red stood a solid sixteen hands at the withers. The girl barely reached the point where his knee rested against Red's flank. Without a word, he leaned out, offered her a hand, and gave her his most charming smile. "My lady."

"First, I need to know something. Which side of the law are you on?"

Trace snorted a laugh and sat back up in the saddle. "Lady, you are some piece of work. Either get up here behind me, or walk. I don't care. But daylight is fading, and I've been riding a long time. I'm ready to get some grub and hit my bedroll." He was losing patience with this woman-child.

Indecision played across her delicate features as she looked at him, then back toward the rock field around them. The curve of her neck above the ruffled collar rose as smooth and pale as alabaster. Trace blinked and looked away.

At last, she turned back to him and sighed. “I’ll accept your offer as long as you promise to be a gentleman.”

He raised an eyebrow. *My offer?*

“I might be a lot of things, but a cad is not one of them. You have my word as a gentleman.” He tipped his hat and settled it back on his head.

Apparently satisfied with his answer, she stretched out a scraped and dirty, fine-boned hand. The nails tiny, ragged pink pearls at the ends of dainty fingers. Trace noticed there wasn’t a gold band where one should be if she was telling the truth about having a husband. He let it go and hoisted her up behind him. A ripple of energy traveled from her hand up his arm. She couldn’t have weighed more than a hundred pounds. *They say dynamite comes in small packages.*

He chuckled to himself and urged the gelding forward. A small gasp came from behind him, and two arms wrapped around his waist. They burned like a brand through his shirt and into his skin. *This is going to be a long few miles.*

Trace tugged down on the brim of his beaver-felt hat, then reached for his Winchester. Instead, his hand found the firm, cloth-covered surface of the girl’s knee.

“Sorry. I need my rifle.”

Without a word, she lifted her leg aside. He pulled the weapon from its scabbard and settled it across the saddle horn. His eyes scanned the hillside and pines, alert to the possibility that the lion hadn’t gone far.

CHAPTER 3

They hadn't gone far when the cowboy started humming a soft tune. The soothing sound beckoned Chloe to rest her weary head against his broad back. She mentally shook herself, determined to remain alert and in control.

"What's that you're humming?"

"It's called *The Cowboy's Lament*."

"Are there words to the song?" she asked.

"Yes. It's about a man who comes on to a young cowboy dying in the streets of Laredo, Texas, from a gunshot wound. The injured cowboy tells the man how he came to be dying and asked him to see that he's buried proper."

"How tragic, to die young and never have a future." She thought of her mother who died at the same age Chloe was now. A yearning for the woman she had no memories of filled her spirit.

"Could you sing it for me?"

At first, she didn't think he was going to comply. Then quietly the deep tenor notes rose as he sang the ballad.

As I walked out in the streets of Laredo
As I walked out in Laredo one day
I spied a young cowboy
all wrapped in white linen

All wrapped in white linen
and cold as the clay
I see by your outfit that you are a cowboy
These words he did say as I boldly stepped by
Come sit down beside me
and hear my sad story
I'm shot in the breast
and I'm going to die
Once in the saddle I used to go dashing
Once in the saddle I used to go gay
But I took to drinkin'
and then to card playin'
Got shot in the breast
and I'm dying today
Oh, beat the drum slowly
and play the fife lowly
Play the dead march as you carry me along
Take me to the green valley,
there lay the sod o'er me
For I'm a young cowboy
and know I've done wrong

The haunting melody brought tears to Chloe's eyes. "How beautiful but sad."

"Yeah, life has a way of kicking you in the teeth when you least expect it." An edge came to the cowboy's voice that she couldn't quite identify. It held a mixture of anger, remorse, and pain.

What had he endured to be so jaded and cynical? She looked at the expanse of his back and wondered what his story was.

"The cabin's that way." She pointed to the trail of smoke rising in the distance. The melancholy of the moment forgotten. With the relief of being back in familiar surroundings, Chloe loosened her grip on the cowboy's waist and let herself relax.

Gray tentacles of smoke curled up from the stone chimney and dissipated into the evening sky. Chief came bounding up to greet them, his shaggy tail wagging his entire body. Chloe had never been so glad to see the big mutt and the little log cabin. Jasper appeared as they ambled across the dirt yard toward the corral.

One hand to the small of his back, the old man winced as he stepped off the stoop and made the slow crossing toward the barn. He pulled the tattered, sweat-stained shape he called a hat from his head. A sparse stand of graying hair sprang loose to sway like drunken twigs all over his round dome.

"Where you been, girly? I was getting a mite worried." He reached up to help Chloe from her perch behind the saddle and let out a low groan. His weathered face screwed up in pain. After he made sure her feet were firmly on the ground, he dropped both hands to his back.

Chloe frowned in concern. He'd been fine when he left for his mining claim that morning. "Are you okay?"

"Not as right as rain, but I'll manage. So tell me what happened."

"I got a little turned around when a big cat started following me."

The cowboy climbed from the saddle to stand beside her. Once again, she was keenly aware of his height and lean, muscular frame.

He worked the reins over the horse's head and let them drop. "Mountain lion a few miles back. Best keep an eye out, J.J."

"Trace Rawlings." Jasper reached out, pumped the cowboy's hand, and patted his back. "You scoundrels back in this territory again?"

So his name is Trace. Chloe liked the sound of it. *It fits him.*

Trace pulled off his hat. The last rays of sun glinted off the coppery strands that lay in a flat swirl on his head. He ran a hand through the dark mess, bringing it to life. "Yeah, it was getting a little hot up north. I'm supposed to meet up with Butch and Sundance at the Bassett Ranch." He glanced back at Chloe. "I got sidetracked."

He gave a gentle punched to the old man's shoulder. "So when did an old bachelor like you decide to tie the knot and how come I wasn't invited to the wedding?"

Jasper looked dumbstruck. Before he could answer, Chloe grabbed up a bucket hanging on the fencepost and headed toward the spring. She didn't want to see the cowboy's face when he learned the truth, and Jasper was sure to set him straight.

"She told you that?" A chuckle started in Jasper's gut and rolled up to a full-blown belly laugh. "I like myself a good, home cooked meal as much as the next man, but not enough to tie the knot again. Laughing Brook was all the woman I'll ever need, rest her soul. No sirree, I plan to go to the great beyond unhitched and carefree." He tittered some more and massaged his lower back. "That there gal is my housekeeper and cook. I got tired of living in a sty, eating trail grub day in and day out, so I put an advertisement in some papers cross Wyoming and down Denver way. She showed up at Jarvie's a month or so ago."

Chloe pumped the bucket full of cool, clear spring water and shuffled toward the cabin. Caught in a lie, she kept her eyes focused on the cabin door and her chin up. She felt her cheeks grow hotter as she passed by the two men.

"You won't be staying for supper, will you, Mr.

Rawlings?" It was more of a statement than a question. Chloe hoped it was true. She had no desire to sit at a table with an outlaw. Especially one that made her skin tingle and her mind go blank.

A strong hand reached out and pulled the full bucket from her, slopping a little on the ground between them. "I'd be mighty obliged for a decent meal and a chance to sit in a chair instead of a saddle for a while, Miss…"

"Cantrell. Chloe Elizabeth Cantrell." Her hands free, she struggled to know what to do with them. She wasn't about to extend her hand in welcome. Smoothing her hair back from her face, she sighed her discomfort. "I guess I owe you an apology, Mr. Rawlings. I lied about being married because I thought it might offer me some protection. I was wrong to assume you would hurt me. For that, I'm sorry."

"No harm done. Can't say I haven't spun a few tales in my day when I saw the need."

She turned to where Jasper stood grinning at the two of them. "You can wipe that silly grin off your face, you old coot. Supper will be ready in half an hour."

Not waiting for a response, she headed toward the squat little structure that had become home.

Trace's long strides carried him past her and into the cabin as if he owned the place. He was already pouring water into a kettle when Chloe stepped into the room. She stopped short, surprised and disconcerted at how much the cowboy filled the space. "I'll just wash up and get the stew on the fire, and then the basin will be free for you to clean up."

She pulled her apron down off a peg by the door and turned to feed wood into the stove, bumping into Trace's bent form.

"Oh, excuse me." Completely flustered, she quickly stepped back, but not before causing Trace to grab the stove to keep himself from falling.

The sound of sizzling skin and the smell of burned flesh was instant.

"Ouch!" Trace yelped and sprang back, holding his hand. His face tensed in pain.

Jasper stepped into the room just in time to see the collision. "Looks like you two are getting to know one another right quick." He snickered as he shuffled to his old Windsor rocker and settled in. "That's gonna leave a nasty burn, Sonny Boy."

Trace plunged his injured hand into the half-full bucket and cursed through clenched teeth.

"Oh, my goodness, I'm so sorry. Here, let me look at that." Chloe moved to examine Trace's injured hand.

"It's fine," he growled and stepped away. The menace in his voice was unmistakable.

"I was just trying to help," Chloe stammered and backed off. Without another word, she moved passed him and tended to the supper preparations. *Insufferable lout.*

~

Trace wasn't surprised Chloe had lied about a husband. He'd come to know old Jasper pretty well over the past nine months or so. Frequent trips to the Hole, now called Brown's Park, offered the opportunity to get acquainted with the old man. The codger contained a gold mine of information. Besides, Trace liked his smart wit and easy-going ways.

Nestled in rugged country right in the corner of Wyoming, Utah, and Colorado, Brown's Park had become a refuge for several gangs of outlaws. Jasper's place was situated just over a couple of ridges from the Bassett Ranch, where Sundance and Butch liked to hide out. It was their halfway point between Hole In The Wall in Wyoming and Robber's Roost in the canyon lands of Utah.

"J.J., you got a clean rag I can tie around this?" He held up his scalded hand, now bright red across the palm and beginning to blister.

"Pretty much everything in here is a rag, but at least they're clean, thanks to Chloe." He pointed to a jumble of scraps of cloth nestled in a crate in the corner. "Help yourself. Too bad that's your shooting hand. Chloe, fetch him that tube of liniment on the shelf there. I use it on old Jake and Jessie when they gets chigger and blowfly bites."

"Here, let me." Chloe stepped forward, and without looking up, grabbed his hand. Trace looked down at the top of her head. Raven black curls glistened in the lamplight and the sweet smell of lilac wafted up to fill him with the memory of his mother's favorite scent. The gnawing pain of her loss and the picture of finding her and his father's bodies momentarily replaced the pain in his hand and the electric spark of the girl's touch.

He had returned home from back east to surprise his parents. Instead, he'd been the one to find their bodies lying cold and lifeless behind the long glass counter of their Austin dry goods store, the cash register and safe both empty. The Colt double-action revolver found next to his father's body now rested in Trace's holster. Law enforcement believed the Black Jack Ketchum gang was responsible for the killings and robbery.

That moment had changed Trace's life forever.

CHAPTER 4

Darkness settled in and encircled the log cabin like a shroud. Chloe had gone to bed behind the curtain that separated her room from the main part of the house. Jasper had fallen asleep in his rocker. His harsh snores punctuated the stillness beyond the makeshift door. She couldn't hear Trace, but the lamp still glowed through the thin fabric that divided the space and kept her from having to face the man.

Unable to sleep, she laid there, staring into the dark. Why did he make her feel so out of kilter, like a landlubber on the deck of a sea-bound ship? She'd never lost sleep over a man before. Oh, there was Jimmy Fallow at school, but he turned out to be a liar and a cheat, running off with Esther Simpson. She'd been a fool to think the stupid boy was the man for her. That was about the time her father decided a finishing school offered a much more proper setting for her. A month later Chloe began attending The Ogontz School for Young Ladies.

Vowing off boys, she concentrated on her schooling and found herself drawn to the arts. Under the tutelage of Miss Margaret Bateman, Chloe discovered her talent for writing and became a feature contributor for the Ogontz Mosaic, the school's monthly periodical. Then, much to her delight, she was selected to play Dolly in their theatrical production of

George Bernard Shaw's play 'You Never Can Tell' in her last year at the school.

Chloe smiled at the memory of her father leading the clapping as she took her bow on opening night. Standing beside him, Lucius Wheeler whistled and clapped, giving her a wink from his second row seat.

Her smile faded at the thought of the man. Fourteen years her senior, he was closer to her father's age than hers. Lucius had always been a gentleman around her, but there was an undercurrent of something Chloe couldn't quite identify that left her uneasy. Back at the factory after graduation and three years of college, she found herself going out of her way to avoid her father's manager. The trip out west had been an excuse to escape his attentions.

Trace Rawlings wasn't like Jimmy or Lucius. At least she didn't think so. There was something different about him. Chloe turned on her side and chewed her lip. Unrecognizable emotions fluttered like butterfly wings across her heart. She pressed her eyes closed, determined to find sleep and chase thoughts of the man in the other room out of her mind. They flew open again when the sounds of horses filtered in from outside.

She slid down off the high bed and tiptoed to the curtain to peek out. The border collie at Trace's feet gave a low growl.

"Shh, Chief." Trace pushed back his chair and opened the door. The lamplight through the two small windows that fronted the cabin cast shadows on the riders still mounted on their horses.

"Hey, Trace, thought we might find you here."

"Yeah, we know how much you dislike the bunk house at the Bassetts." Another voice chimed out from the darkness.

"It's not the bunkhouse, I mind. It's the smell of all your stinky feet and the God awful snoring. I'm good here. Why don't you boys ride on over there? Josie's liable to have a big pot of beans and meat still simmering." Trace leaned against the doorframe, his wrapped hand braced above his head.

"What happened?" came the question from the first voice.

Trace wagged his fingers. "Got a little too close to the fire."

Chloe heard the creak of someone climbing down out of the saddle. Chief growled again and moved to sit next to Trace guarding the entrance.

Good dog. Her stomach churned at the thought of more strange men spending the night in the small cabin. Surely, Jasper would wake up and send them on their way. She looked over at the sleeping figure. Dead to the world, the old man's head lay back, his mouth hanging open. A rough snore confirmed her fears.

Should she throw on her clothes and march out there herself to demand they leave? Chloe pressed against the wall and chewed her lip in indecision.

A third voice carried in from outside. His tone was low and somehow threatening. The skin on her arms and on the back of her neck instantly prickled. She moved to stand back next to the curtain and pulled the edge aside to allow one eye to peek out.

"The law's been on our trail for most of yesterday and today. We've been moving hard and fast. Lost them down the shoots in the canyon. We're ready to call it a night, right boys?"

Trace straightened and blocked the only entrance. Impressing Chloe with how his broad shoulders filled the space. *Please make them go away.*

"The barn's got clean straw laid down. You can put your horses in the corral. Sorry there's no grub, J. J. wasn't expecting company." He reached across to the counter and lifted a cloth-wrapped loaf of bread that he tossed out the door. “Fresh bread though, that will have to do.”

“I ain’t ever knowed Jasper to make bread before. He got him a woman in there?”

Someone snickered. “Didn’t think old Jasper had it in him. Think maybe he’d be willing to share? We could use a little something to keep us warm tonight.”

Chloe let out an audible gasp. Trace’s back stiffened and tensed under his clean, chambray shirt. One hand dropped behind him, fingers splayed in warning. The ruff of fur around Chief’s neck and along his back stood up. His displeasure sounded from his throat and showed in his bared teeth.

Trace snorted. “Don’t know any woman willing to put up with that old rascal. He’s got himself down in the back, so I’m staying here. The bread is my doing so no complaints if it’s heavy and chewy.”

Chloe’s own back stiffened. Was he saying her bread wasn’t any good? How dare he after eating almost a whole loaf all by himself. She had a mind to walk right out there and give him ‘what for’ as Auntie Clare would say. After all, she’d learned to make bread and every other kind of cooking at the feet of a master. Clare Morrison was renowned for the delicious dinners she prepared for Papa’s dinner parties.

Ready to do battle, she was about to pull the curtain back when Trace stepped outside and closed the door behind him. Chief whined and scratched to join him.

~

Trace wasn’t about to let either of the Logan brothers or Walt Putnam near Chloe. Where the protective streak came from, he didn’t know. Maybe she reminded him of Pamela and Myrna, the two sisters he’d lost to cholera when they were small.

He heard her behind him. Not sure she would stay put, he stepped out onto the stoop. A match to the wick of a lantern hanging by the door illuminated the three weary cowboys. They looked as done in as he felt. The muzzles of their horses almost grazed the ground, spent after a hard days' ride. Trace relaxed. Outlaws or not, these men and their mounts were in no condition to cause trouble—not tonight, anyway.

He handed the lantern to Harvey "Kid Curry" Logan. Known for his short fuse and long memory, the man emanated distrust. Losing his brother Johnnie in an 1896 shootout with Montana rancher, James Winters, had hardened Logan and turned him into a cold-hearted killer.

From the first day they'd met, it had taken everything in Trace to hold back and not provoke a gunfight. He was on the short list of possible men responsible for his parent's murders and for months, Trace had been gathering the evidence to confirm his suspicions. When that happened, the guns would come out.

Even though they rode together, he learned early on not to turn his back on the man. Tonight, his instincts told him the trio would be harmless unless cornered. "I expect to be leaving in a day or two. As soon as I get J. J. situated with firewood and water, and Red has a chance to rest. Butch and Sundance should be at the Bassetts already and I suspect the rest will be riding in tomorrow sometime."

"We ain't hanging around to chop firewood. We'll be heading out by sunrise." The Kid grabbed up the reins of his horse and turned toward the weathered barn that listed to the south like a tired soldier. The other two followed him, bone weary and saddle sore.

Trace would make sure they were gone before Chloe woke up, which meant he needed to get some sleep if he wanted to be up by dawn.

“See ya’ all Saturday morning,” he called out. Once the barn door closed behind them, Trace stepped back into the house. His eye caught the movement of the curtain covering the door of Chloe’s room—the one he normally slept in when he stayed here.

“Good night, Miss Cantrell.”

When she didn’t answer, he moved to the small adjacent bedroom where J.J.’s lumpy mattress beckoned him. Exhausting him both physically and mentally, the charade he’d been playing was exacting a high price to his soul. *I won’t quit until justice is served, no matter the cost.*

CHAPTER 5

Chloe woke to the sound of an axe striking and splitting wood. She grabbed up her robe and peeked around the curtain partition. Jasper and Trace were both gone, the room empty. She caught motion through the window and tiptoed closer. She noticed the small corral stood empty, the extra horses gone. *Thank you, Lord.*

Jasper sat on the gray weathered trunk of a cottonwood packing tobacco into the bowl of his pipe. Every time Chloe watched him do that, she thought of her father. Would she ever get over missing the man who dominated her life?

Trace, chest bare and glistening with sweat, swung the axe down on a short section of a log standing on end on an ancient stump. One handed, the axe and the strength behind it cleaved the wood in two like a knife through melted butter. If he could do that with one hand, what was he capable of with two?

Mesmerized by the ripple of muscle bulging and knotting across Trace's back, it took Chloe a moment to realize the two men were speaking about her. Someone had propped the window beside her open a couple of inches to let in the fresh morning air. It also allowed their words to drift in with the breeze.

"She's looking for a man," Jasper announced around the

stem of his pipe. “A fellow name Harry Longabaugh,”

Trace tensed and stopped mid-swing. “What’s a woman like her want with the likes of Harry?” He finished the swing, burying the axe blade almost to the hilt. “You think she’s another one of the scorned women he seems to leave in his wake everywhere he goes?”

“Nay, she’s not his type. Sides, she’s good folk—decent, and God-fearing. Her pa brought her up right. Ma died when she was a little thing. Raised by a free woman and her pa. Man died a few months back. That’s about all I’ve gotten out of her.”

Chloe stood frozen, eager to hear more about this Harry. Could they be talking about her half-brother? She’d spent the past four months trying to determine his whereabouts. Notes found in her father’s desk sent her to Denver. There she found a man who told her to head to Rock Springs, Wyoming. Chloe had immediately bought a ticket on the next westbound train. The journey from Denver took her through breath-taking country and deposited her in the high desert town.

Rock Springs proved to be a rough and tumble place with clapboard buildings and a wide dirt street that ran through the middle of it. A church anchored one end while a two-story brick building housing The Cosgriff Hotel welcomed visitors at the other end.

For several days, Chloe ventured in and out of various establishments, where she heard rumors of a cowboy who went by the name of Harry Long. Could he have shortened his name? Her inquiries garnered a slew of strange looks and a handful of warnings. The best clue she got was that this ne’er-do-well hung out in a secluded place across the state line called Brown’s Park, and that he went by a nickname. What that nickname was, no one would say.

Providence—or the Lord—guided her to the newspaper

advertisement in the Rock Springs Miner, about a man in Brown's Park needing a housekeeper and cook. On faith, Chloe secured passage on the next freight wagon heading south. The sixty-five-mile trip was excruciating. For two long days, she sat next to the driver and endured the hard wood bench not meant for comfort.

"So you're gonna work for Jasper Johnson, are ya?" The storekeeper, John Jarvie, grinned and shook his head. He looked her up and down. "Don't take this the wrong way, miss, but you don't exactly look like cow country housekeeper material."

Chloe did her best to smooth her rumpled traveling suit and stand tall. "I'm quite capable of keeping house and cooking. I assure you, Mr. Johnson will not find me wanting."

Jarvie pulled a pocket watch from his vest. "Well then, I'll wish you luck and send you on your way." He pointed to a thin cloud of dust in the distance. "That be Jasper, I reckon."

When Jasper Johnson showed up at the Lodore store in a weathered buckboard, Chloe was sure she'd made a terrible mistake. The disheveled man squinted at her from his high seat, a pipe clenched between yellowed teeth. He harrumphed loudly, then climbed down, slapping dust from his ragged clothes with a tattered, sweat-stained felt hat. Apparently satisfied, he smashed the mangled headgear back on his freckled head. It perched there above a weathered, leathery face that reminded her of the faces her father would carve for her out of old, wrinkled pine knots. Where was the country gentleman mentioned in the ad?

After looking each other up and down a few times, Mr. Johnson gave her a lopsided grin and hoisted her carpet bag into the back. "You're mighty young, but I guess you'll do." He extended a dirt-encrusted hand. "Name's Johnson, but you can call me Jasper or J.J."

Chloe forced a smile and grimaced at touching the filthy paw he held out to her. "Chloe Elizabeth Cantrell." Had she made a monumental mistake answering that ad?

Uncertainty churned in her stomach on the long ride back and turned to dismay when she saw the small, squat cabin surrounded by sagebrush and scrub oak. It didn't look in the least bit welcoming and was nothing like she'd envisioned.

That had been one of her first lessons in not trusting appearances. Jasper proved to have a sweet, gentle soul under that gruff, dirty exterior. Once he cleaned up, he didn't look or smell half bad, and reminded her of her Grandpa Joe.

Tears sprang to her eyes at the thought of the loved ones she'd lost. She brushed them away with an impatient hand. Tears would not help her accomplish her mission. She took a deep breath and leaned closer to the open window, anxious to hear any tidbits of information she could procure.

~

The idea that Chloe was somehow tied up with Sundance made Trace clench his jaw and pull his mouth into a grim, hard line. He needed details. He looked back at the cabin. The flour sack curtain fluttered. Had she been eavesdropping on their conversation? Who was this girl who seemed such a contradiction?

Determined to get some answers, Trace put on his shirt. In a few long strides, he reached the cabin door and flung it open.

Chloe gasped and stepped back, clutching the neck of her robe. "I was just putting some water on." To support her statement, she reached for the kettle. Her hair made a lump under the back of the robe as if she put it on in a hurry.

"So what is a city girl like you doing out here in the Wild West?" he asked as he swung a chair around and straddled it backwards, ignoring her discomfort.

"What makes you think I'm from the city?" She turned and crossed her arms.

He couldn't help the snort. Was she serious? It had been a long time since he'd seen someone so out of their element. "Just a good guess. I mean, you don't exactly look like the typical frontier woman." He rested his arms across the chair back. "So?"

She busied herself dropping lard into a cast-iron skillet. "If you must know, I'm here on business. I need to find a man. Mr. Johnson was kind enough to give me employment while I search."

Trace watched her expertly crack several eggs into a blue speckled bowl and begin whipping them. "J.J. said you asked him about a Harry Longabaugh. How do you know him?"

As if she just realized she was still in her nightclothes, Chloe pushed a wooden spoon at him and headed to her room. "That, sir, is none of your business. Stir the eggs while I get dressed." From behind the curtain, she added. "And don't let them burn. Jasper likes them fluffy and light."

Trace chuckled and got up. He used the wooden spoon and moved the eggs around. "Got any bacon to go with these eggs?"

"Right here." J.J. held up a slab of bacon as he stepped in the door. "Josie brought it over yesterday. I stored it out in the springhouse to make it last."

Chloe came back into the room, tying her apron around a slim waist. "I'll take that." With the bacon in one hand, she relieved Trace of the spoon. "If you two want bacon with your eggs, I'll need more wood to stoke the fire."

When she turned her back to him, he couldn't help but be impressed by the glossy, black sheet of hair that flowed down to her waist. The sight made him forget what he was doing and brought a sudden heat to his body. "I'll bring some in. I need to feed Red, anyway." He made for the door and cool, fresh air.

"Are you leaving?" she asked.

He couldn't miss that look of relief on her face. He pulled the door opened and grabbed his hat from the row of pegs. "Only as far as the barn. There're some chores need doing, and J.J.'s back needs rest. I'll be leaving in the morning right after breakfast." He gave her a firm look. "I'm looking for a man, too."

CHAPTER 6

Once breakfast was over, Chloe didn't see Trace for the rest of the morning, except from a distance. She watched from the stoop as he did repairs on the barn roof. The dilapidated, weather-beaten structure didn't look worth saving. Still, Trace seemed determined to keep it watertight and dry for the two mules and a handful of chickens that called it home.

She was pulling lunch from the oven when he came in at noon. Sweat stained his shirt and marked his forehead where hat met skin. He permeated the room with the musky, animal smell of the barnyard.

"Goodness, couldn't you have washed up first?" Chloe waved a hand in front of her nose and made a face.

Trace stopped in his tracks. "Sorry, guess I'm not used to eating in a civilized fashion when I'm at J.J.'s." He turned toward the door. "I'll just head down to the spring. Where's the old man, anyway?"

"In the root cellar getting me a jar of preserves for the bread. Of course, you don't have to have any since you think it's heavy and chewy."

"I figured you must have heard my comment last night. I lied to throw those guys off. They didn't need to know you were here."

She set the steamy pan on the stovetop and gave him a half-smile. “I know how good my bread is.” She swished a potholder at him. “Don’t doddle. Shepherd’s pie is best when it’s hot.”

Tyler grinned back. “If it tastes as good as it smells I’ll be back in two shakes of a lamb’s tail.” He took one more deep breath in and licked his lips. “Make that one shake.” With that, he hustled out the door.

From the window, Chloe watched him move across the yard. His long strides ate up the ground and emphasized that masculine self-assurance some men seemed to come by naturally.

He’s certainly very male.

~

Chase set back, his bandaged hand resting on his stomach. “That was the best meal I’ve had since I sat at my mother’s table. My compliments to the chef.” He gave Chloe a half smile and tipped a non-existent hat. “Where did you learn to cook like that?”

His words brought a blush of rose to her cheeks. She dipped her head and smiled.

She’s really quite lovely.

“The woman who raised me, Auntie Clare, doesn’t think any girl worth her salt can be a proper wife unless she knows how to cook and bake.”

“Where’s your ma?” he asked.

Chloe looked up at him. Sadness flickered across her eyes and disappeared. “She died when I was three. Clare worked for my parents. She was born a slave at a big plantation house down in Georgia. She came north on the underground railroad with her beau just before the start of the civil war in ’61. He didn’t make it.

"My father was a strong supporter of the abolitionist movement and when Clare showed up in Philadelphia, he found her a job. After the war, my father met and married my mother. When she needed help, he remembered the runaway slave he'd rescued. Clare had married Abel Morrison by then and was pregnant with their first son, Matthew. They all ended up coming to live with us. Clare, Abel and their two boys have been with us—me, all my life. They're all the family I have."

"You miss them."

A sad smile pulled at the corners of Chloe's mouth. "Very much."

Trace knew the kind of longing for family that she felt. Being an orphan at any age was tough. Losing the connection with people that knew all your faults and still loved you weighed on him heavily since the murders of his parents.

Wanting to bring a smile back to her face, he changed the subject. "Surely you have a beau back home. What does he think of you gallivanting across the country all by yourself?"

Chloe's chin came up. The smile he anticipated became a firm line across her full lips instead. "I assure you, Mr. Rawlings, I am not some ditzy female on a frivolous jaunt to see the west. I'm here on business, and I can take perfectly good care of myself, thank you."

She stood and began clearing the table.

Jasper, quiet this whole time, chuckled. "You got her riled up now. I think I'll just go fetch some more water."

Trace put a hand on the old man's shoulder and stood. "No, you stay here and rest. I'll get the water."

He looked at Chloe's stiff back as she busied herself at the stove. "Just be careful, Miss Cantrell. The west isn't as refined and polite as back East. My advice is to hire someone to handle your business and go back to Philadelphia where you belong."

She swung around. With her arms crossed, she glared at him. “Thank you for your unsolicited opinion, but I’m a grown woman and quite capable of managing my own affairs. Men don’t have a corner on the market when it comes to business, you know.”

Trace rolled his eyes at J.J. and shook his head. Without another word, he headed out the door.

“I think I’ll just sit outside in the shade.” The old man followed him. “It’s a little hot in there, iffin’ you know what I mean.”

Trace huffed. “And I thought you were cantankerous.” He grabbed up the bucket and headed toward the spring. “Women.” He muttered to himself.

CHAPTER 7

The rest of the day Chloe stewed. What was it with men, anyway? Even her own father didn't think her capable enough to handle her own affairs. He loved her—that much she was sure of. But sometimes he'd been blinded by the fact that she was a woman.

Like that should make a difference.

Over the past four years, it became obvious he thought she needed a husband. He invited any number of eligible young men to their home under the pretense of business. They were all nice enough, and Chloe did her best to show interest, but something was always missing. None of them challenged her. There was no spark—at least on her part.

She thought of Lucius. The man didn't know how to take no for an answer. Since her father's death, he'd become relentless in his pursuit of her. If she were honest, he was the primary reason she took on the quest of finding her brother. Her father never intended for her to physically search for him herself, and yet here she was in the middle of the Wild West doing just that.

"I'll show them all I can do this," she muttered to herself as she walked the ridge above the cabin. "I don't need a man."

She brought her chin up in defiance. "Lord, help me be a

Deborah or an Esther."

She smiled at the thought of her two favorite Bible characters; Deborah the judge, and Esther the queen. These two women were smart and courageous. They stepped up when men were afraid to.

Something on the opposite hill caught Chloe's attention. She stopped and shielded her eyes. A blur of gold moved through the sage, making its way down the incline. The mountain lion! She followed its intended path down the hillside to the spring where Jasper kneeled. He seemed focused on something along the water's edge and didn't realize the approaching danger.

Chloe shouted, "Jasper, above you!"

Her voice, carried on the wind, died before it reached him.

"Sweet Jesus, please protect him!"

The prayer was real and said with urgency. She could do nothing from this distance. Gathering her skirt, she hurried down the sloping path.

Trace stepped from the barn, Chief at his heels.

"Trace," she shouted. "The lion is back!" She pointed as he turned his attention toward her.

In an instant, he took in the scene as the cat eased down the slope above the unsuspecting old man. He disappeared for a second and returned with a rifle. At a full out sprint, Trace ran toward Jasper. Chief saw the cougar and bound off in front of him at a dead run, barking and growling at the intruder.

Chloe could only watch in horror. Distracted by the dog, the cat paused on a shelf of rock above where Jasper struggled to his feet trying to figure out what all the commotion was about. The old man looked back at the dog and the man racing toward him and then up at the hillside above him where Trace pointed.

Chloe screamed as Jasper's feet slipped on the muddy

bank and he went down in a heap. Ignoring the threat of the dog charging in his direction, the mountain lion crouched and sprang in one fluid motion.

~

Trace skidded to a stop and swung the rifle up. His fingers stiff under the cloth bandage, he struggled to pull the trigger. *Lord, direct my aim!*

He fired. The gun recoiled against his shoulder. Without waiting to see if the shot found its target, he levered the spent casing out and fired again.

Jasper lay unmoving, the hundred and fifty-pound cat on top of him. Chief reached the pair before Trace was halfway across the yard. The big mutt attacked the lion without hesitation. Snarling and biting, the dog tugged and worried the animal's exposed neck.

Trace fell to his knees and pushed him away. "Easy, boy. Good dog." He heaved the heavy body of the cat off to one side. "J.J.—come on, old man—talk to me."

The target was obviously down, but Trace worried that one of his shots might have hit his friend. Gently, he rolled Jasper over and did a quick search for a bloody hole. Relief flooded his body when the old man groaned and lifted a hand to clutch Trace's sleeve. Chief crowded in and began licking his owner's face. His whole body wiggling, he whimpered his excitement.

"Get off me, you crazy mutt." Jasper sputtered and screwed up his face against the exuberant tongue washing he was being given.

"He's just relieved you're okay. You are okay, aren't you?" Trace asked.

J.J. looked over at the still form. A bullet hole to the inside of one shoulder and another a few inches lower in the chest marred the cat's golden coat. "By golly, I wouldn't have been iffin' you hadn't stopped that big fella. Couldn't have asked for a prettier shot than that, I be thinkin'. Looks like I'm gonna have me a right fine rug to warm my feet on."

Chloe ran up and collapsed next to the pair. She gathered Jasper's face between her small hands and made him look at her. "Are you okay? I shouted a warning, but you didn't hear me."

She turned to Trace. "Thank God you did."

"I could have never made that shot with this hand." He held up his injured hand. The bandage was loose and dirty. "I think God had more to do with it than I did."

Chloe gave him a strange look then turned back to J.J. "Let's get you up and inside where you can rest."

"Aw shucks, girlie, it'd take more than an ornery old puma to best the likes of Jasper B. Johnson." He shrugged out of her grasp and turned to Trace. "Want to give me a hand skinning this here critter? Laughing Brook showed me how to tan the hide years ago and the meat will be mighty tasty."

Trace couldn't help but make a face. Shooting an animal about to attack someone was one thing. Pulling out the innards and chopping it up was another. "Guess this would set you up for meat for a while, huh?"

J.J. bent over and lifted the head. "Surely will. Chloe girl, we're gonna have us some lion steaks tonight."

Trace watched Chloe blanch. She paled and put a hand to her mouth. Poor girl, she's probably never seen an animal butchered. Steak on the table, medium rare was more her style.

"Why don't you go on up to the house?"

He turned to J.J. "I'll go get the handcart, and we'll move the carcass to the barn where it's cool."

Chloe only gave a nod of agreement and hurried off to the cabin. Trace wished he could join her.

SECOND CHANCES

CHAPTER 8

For the rest of the day, Chloe avoided the barn where the two men were busy with their bloody task. The thought of butchering the beautiful animal made her stomach roll. Yet she understood Jasper's excitement. The wilderness was no place to be squeamish. Once again, she realized how ill-prepared she was to live on the frontier.

Determined to make herself useful, she decides to tackle the arduous chore of doing the laundry. The shade under the boughs of Jasper's lone cottonwood offered the perfect place to set up her washtubs and keep her out of the sun's heat. The solitary chore gave her time to think about the overheard conversation from that morning. She couldn't understand why they weren't willing to talk about Harry. What was it about this mystery man that no one was willing to share information with her?

She stood pegging the wet clothes along a makeshift line and watched Trace come towards her. He looked like some kind of warrior coming back from a bloody battle, his britches and shirtfront stained with dark blood. The bandage on his hand was no longer white and a smear of something nasty ran across his cheek.

"I still have water in the washtub. If you want to give me

those clothes, I'll wash them up for you."

Trace looked down at himself. "Yeah, I look like I wallowed in the stuff, don't I? I'll just wash up in the house and change into clean clothes. Thanks for the offer, but you don't have to take care of me. Just leave the tub full and I'll do them myself."

Chloe shrugged her shoulders. "Suit yourself. There's hot water on the stove."

Determined to get some answers, she waited until he returned and then pretended to be busy folding the few things that were already dry.

"Where's Jasper? I imagine he looks about as bad as you did."

Trace chuckled. "He's in there doing some kind of ceremony to thank the cat for providing food—like it had a choice. He wore a leather apron and sleeve covers, so he managed to stay pretty clean." He dumped the bloody clothes in the tub and moved to pick up the stout stick Chloe used to move them around in the hot water.

"Here, let me help you. You don't need to get that hand wet." She took the paddle from him and began pushing the clothes around. "It's not hot anymore anyway, which is good. Hot water would set the stains."

She nodded toward his injured hand, the dirty bandage a sharp contrast to his cleaned up appearance. "When we get done here, I'll change that for you. You need to keep it clean to avoid infection."

Trace held his hand up. "You're probably right."

She dropped the stick and tugged his sopping pants to the washboard. The wet canvas britches were heavy and awkward as she pushed and pulled them up and down the rough surface. "Can I ask you something?"

"Sure, but I might not have an answer."

"You said God helped you make that shot. Do you really believe that?"

Trace ran his good hand through his damp hair, creating rusty brown waves. One curl fell across his forehead. Chloe fought the urge to smooth it back into place. She swallowed and looked away.

"Sure, why not? Don't you believe in God?" He moved to lean against the broad tree trunk.

"Of course, I'm just surprised you do, being an outlaw and everything." She went back to scrubbing the clothes, relieved he'd moved away. She couldn't think clearly when he stood so close.

Trace pushed off the tree and crossed his arms. "Pious rich folks don't have the corner market on God, you know. I was raised in church and still attend when I have the opportunity. I may be a sinner in your eyes, but Jesus knows who I am inside."

Chloe could see by his stiff posture she'd touched a sore spot with him and changed the subject. "Is Harry an outlaw like you? Is that how you know him?"

She watched his face, sure she'd know if he was hiding something. His stony expression didn't change.

"I know a few Harrys. Why?"

Chloe wrangled the dripping pants over the line and pegged the legs in place. "I heard you and Jasper talking this morning. He told you I'm looking for Harry Longabaugh. Do you know him?"

"Hey there, you two, ready to grill up these here steaks?" Jasper came up carrying a couple of thick slabs of meat.

Chloe waited for Trace to answer her.

He moved past her to join Jasper. "Can't say that I do."

He was lying. She was sure of it. Hadn't he admitted the day before that he lied on occasion? Chloe hung the shirt next to the pants, wiped her hands on her apron, and followed the men into the house. One question nagged at her. Did Trace know Harry because her brother was an outlaw like him?

~

Thankful the grisly job was done. Trace would enjoy the steaks, but the butchering was something he'd never had a stomach for. Much like the lying.

Not sure why he told Chloe he didn't know Harry, he had to admit it bothered him that she was somehow tied to the outlaw. Few people knew that Sundance Kid's real name was Harry Longabaugh. What was her connection? *She'll just have to find out for herself. I'm not going to help her.*

The trio gathered round the table. Fat, juicy steaks covered their plates. Trace could see Chloe was uncomfortable with eating the meat the cougar supplied. He didn't get much satisfaction with eating the beautiful animal either, but he wasn't one to turn down a steak, no matter where it came from.

"Mr. Rawlings, would you like to say grace?" she asked. He could see the challenge in her eyes.

He gave her a half smile. "It would be my pleasure, Miss Cantrell."

Jasper reached out from his side of the table and grabbed up Chloe's hand. He held his paw out to Trace. "Iffin' you're gonna bless this here food, I say we do it proper."

Trace curled his fingers around Chloe's, thankful he could bow his head. He expected her skin to be soft and smooth. Instead, it was wrinkled and rough from the hot water and the scrubbing. She sure was a puzzle. Spoiled and privileged maybe, but he'd yet to hear her complain. Again, he wondered about her connection to Sundance.

CHAPTER 9

Chloe stood at the sink and strained to hear the conversation outside. Auntie Clare would have given her a lecture about eavesdropping had she been there. She didn't care. Learning more about her brother took precedent over good manners. She wished she had thought to open the window further before the men walked up. Instead, she leaned close and lifted a corner of the curtain.

Trace stood beside his horse. "You need to talk her into going home, J.J.. She's not cut out for this life."

Jasper pushed his hat back and scratched his head. "Grown mighty fond of the little gal, but you're probably right. Just don't know iffin' she'll give up until she finds Harry." He chuckled. "She can be a pretty persistent little thing."

Trace huffed. "Spoiled and used to getting her own way is probably closer to the truth."

Chloe gave her own soft snort. *The man wouldn't know the truth if it slapped him in the face.*

"I'm meeting up with the boys at the Bassets this morning. The plan is to head out tomorrow. You should be good for firewood and I patched the barn roof as best I could."

As Chloe watched, Trace shook the old man's hand. They gave each other a manly pat on the back, then stepped apart.

Effortlessly, he swung up into the saddle. He looked good up there, solid and strong. The white of the clean bandage stood out against the shadows of the tree behind him. He waved and swung the horse around.

"Don't be a stranger," Jasper called to the cowboy's retreating back.

Trace waved and nudged the roan into an easy canter.

Chloe let the curtain fall back into place and plunged her hands back into the soapy water. Trace was meeting up with the boys. Would Harry be there, too? This might be the lead she was looking for. Trace knew Harry. She could tell by his reaction when Jasper mentioned him. If only she could follow him. But how?

She finished the dishes and set about sweeping the floor. Somehow, she had to figure out a way to get to the Basset ranch while the men were still there. Once they left, she would lose her chance to finally meet her brother.

She spent the morning doing chores and hatching elaborate schemes. Finally, after lunch, Chloe knew what she was going to do. Her father always said the best plan was the simplest one. Determined to follow his advice, she hung up the damp dishtowel and dried her hands on her apron. She turned to where the old man sat, a happy smile on his face after having eaten another lion steak for breakfast.

"Jasper, do you think Josie and Ann might have the makings for a cake? I was thinking I'd like to bake a chocolate cake, but I'm short on sugar and cocoa." If anything could get Jasper's attention, it was to tempt his sweet tooth.

"A chocolate cake, you say?" He rubbed his stomach. "I ain't had me no kinda cake in nigh on a coon's age. I'll saddle up old Jake and ride over for ya."

That didn't fit into Chloe's plan. She needed to be the one to go, or at least ride along. "You know, I could use a little female time. Why don't you hitch up the buckboard, and I'll ride along? It will give me a chance to chat with the sisters. If they don't have what I need we can go on to Jarvie's store."

A little over an hour later, they were riding into the yard at the Bassett ranch. It sat in a much prettier location, with a beautiful meadow spread out before it and a picturesque view of the sheer, red canyon walls known as the 'Gates of Lodore'. The large, well-constructed log house took advantage of the beautiful scene with a bank of south-facing windows. Everything about the place spoke of planning, care, and prosperity.

Chloe counted an even dozen horses in the corral, including Trace's roan. Another handful grazed in the vast meadow with at least a hundred cows. It created a pretty, peaceful scene. Josie waved as they came into view. A couple of large, hairy dogs came barking to greet them. Three men stepped from the bunkhouse, all with weapons drawn. Two others rested rifles along the top rail of the corral fence where they'd been currying their horses.

"Easy, boys, it's just local company. Howdy, Jasper, you old coot," Josie hollered and followed the dogs up to the wagon as it pulled into the yard under the shade of a pair of giant cottonwoods. She reached a hand up to help Chloe down. "You still cooking for this crazy old man?"

Josephine Bassett, only three years her senior, seemed so much older to Chloe. Dressed in baggy men's work clothes and a wide-brimmed cowboy hat, it was hard to see the lovely woman underneath. Not as stunning as her older sister Ann, Josie could still turn heads. Her winning smile and the mischievous twinkle in her eye seemed to attract men to her like moths to a flame. Chloe wished she had the ease and confidence around men as the two sisters.

"Hi, Josie, hope this is a good time for a visit. Looks like you already have plenty of company." Chloe climbed down from her perch on the buckboard's only seat.

Josie waved a dismissive hand at the men, their guns still at the ready. "Yeah, they've been straggling in the last couple of days. Annie's out hunting with Butch and a couple of the boys. Takes a lot to feed this crowd." Josie wrapped an arm around Chloe's waist. "She'll be sorry she missed you. Come on inside. I have a fresh pot of coffee brewing if these honchos haven't drunk it all."

"You ladies don't worry about me. I'll just mosey on over to my favorite log." Jasper worked his way down off the wagon and moved in the opposite direction, a tail-wagging dog on either side.

Amos Herbert Bassett stepped off the front porch and headed their direction. "Miss Cantrell." The senior Bassett gave a slight bow as he stopped in front of the two women. "Welcome. You picked a lovely day to visit."

The genteel, quiet nature of the older man always amazed Chloe. He was the complete opposite of his children, and from what she gathered, nothing like his late wife. Content to let his wife, Eliza, run the ranch, Herb Bassett lived for his library and music. He was also deeply religious. His late wife's firm hand had kept the children in line and made the ranch a success.

In the seven years since she'd passed, he'd done his best to raise his three sons and two daughters. However, he lacked that no-nonsense authority needed to keep the five young people in line. With his open welcome to any, and all travelers—no matter their caliber, it was no wonder his children were such free spirits.

Chloe thought of Trace Rawlings and the men pointing guns at them as they rode up. What kind of men were they? God-fearing? Certainly not. Killers and thieves? Probably. She determined to keep her distance, especially from her tall, dark rescuer.

"Thank you, Mr. Bassett. It's nice to get out of our own four walls once in a while, especially on such a lovely day."

"Well, you two have a nice visit. I'm going to go jaw with Jasper some." With that, he doffed an invisible hat and moved off.

The two women stepped into the cool interior of the house. It took a minute for Chloe's eyes to adjust to the relative gloom after the bright sunshine. Dust particles danced on the sunlight filtering through the windows and warming the wood floor. A tabby lay curled on the braid rug in the center of one sunny beam. She loved the homey feel of the big, open room with its chinked log walls and large stone fireplace. It was a far cry from Jasper's humble three-room cabin. She carried the steaming cup of strong coffee Josie handed her to the long plank table and was about to sit down when the door burst open and Trace strode in. Why did he always entered a room like he owned the place? His tall, broad-shouldered frame instantly dominated the living space.

"What are you doing here?" His intense blue eyes glinted with anger.

"I take it you two have met." Josie lifted a curious, winged eyebrow.

Chloe set the mug down, put her hands on her hips, and raised her chin. "I came to see Josie. What are *you* doing here?"

Trace's mouth thinned to a hard, flat line. "To use your own words—none of your business."

Josie laced an arm through Chloe's and smiled at Trace. "He's a hot commodity right now. Aren't you, Trace? That seems to be the only time we see these guys in this part of the country." She looked from Chloe to Trace and back again. Her brown eyes lit up with a mischievous twinkle. “I have a wonderful idea! Since we have a house full of company, let’s have a party—here—tonight. Ann and Butch will be bringing in fresh meat. There are potatoes and green beans in the root cellar. I just churned some butter yesterday. The garden is bursting with strawberries that need eating, and we can make some biscuits and a cake for dessert.” She turned to Chloe. “Did Jasper bring his fiddle?”

“Of course, you know he doesn’t go visiting without it.”

The hard line of Trace’s mouth didn’t ease. If anything, it got stiffer. “You really think that’s a good idea? The gang are wired a little tight right now.”

Josie laughed and pushed passed him. “That’s exactly why we should relax and have some fun. You especially, you’re always on edge about something.” She moved out the door to the lip of the porch and hollered toward the corral where the two rifle-toting men were back to currying their horses.

“Boys, we’re having us a hoe down tonight. Set up some kind of table out there under the trees and carry some firewood over to the pit there. Oh and don’t forget to rig up a roasting spit. We’re going to cook up some venison or beef, whatever kind of meat Butch and Ann bring in. Ya’ all are in for a special treat—Chloe’s going to bake one of her delicious cakes and maybe I can talk her into a pie or two.”

Chloe heard a couple of excited exclamations at the announcement, leaving her anything but thrilled. This wasn’t how she planned it at all. She’d hope to get some more information about this Harry she overheard Trace and Jasper talking about, not spend the afternoon cooking and baking for a bunch of questionable characters.

A new thought caused her heart to beat faster, and she caught her breath. What if Harry was one of the guests? What if she was going to meet her brother tonight!

~

Trace found himself less than pleased when he came from the barn and saw J.J. settled on a log in the shade, carrying on an animated conversation with Herb Bassett. What was the old man doing here? Was Chloe with him? His eye caught a flash of dove gray skirt disappearing through the door. The same soft color Chloe wore that morning. His groan turned to a growl. He couldn't allow this girl to get in the way of his plan. He'd worked too long and sacrificed too much to have her muddle things up now. He would have to get her to leave before the others returned. In a few determined strides, he stepped onto the porch and into the house.

Chloe was an unknown commodity, but Trace had no doubt he could persuade her to leave. Josie was a whole other story. This woman could best most men and outside of her sister, she could outride and out shoot them as well. He had never met anyone quite like the Bassett sisters. Good-looking and cultured when they wanted to be, they were just as at ease with the most rugged outlaw. The two women together made a handsome and formidable pair.

Trace knew he'd lost the battle the minute Josie linked arms with Chloe. Without admitting defeat, he stomped out of the room and went to join J.J. and Herb Bassett. Maybe he could persuade the old man into taking the girl home.

The tall, thin form of the Bassett patriarch unfolded from his place on the log. "Come join us, son."

Trace paced in front of them and rubbed the back of his neck, too irritated to sit still.

"What's got you so riled up? You look like a bear that got poked one too many times with a stick." J.J. joked.

"Just not in the mood for a party, I guess. You know they'll bring out that rot gut Ann calls moonshine." He turned to Mr. Bassett. "No offense, sir, but it could get mighty rowdy around here. Sundance will be back from Jarvie's by then and Butch said earlier that they expect a few more boys in later this afternoon."

"A shindig, huh? Glad I brought my fiddle." J.J. ran a hand down the front of his worn shirtfront. "Wished I'd wore my Sunday-go-to-meeting clothes. Got to look swanky for the ladies." He tittered and slapped a knee.

Herb worked a hand through the flow of his full, gray-speckled beard and adjusted the wire-framed glasses that perched on his nose, a habit he had when he was thinking. "It's been a while since we had some enjoyment to distract us, what with fence mending, moving cattle, and such. Too bad Sam, Elbert, and George aren't here. Them boys of mine love to dance.

"Tell you what, I'll see that Ann limits the liquor until afterwards. I don't abide drinking myself, you know. I suppose Josie and Chloe are already in there baking up a storm." His long-fingered hands patted his vest-covered stomach. "I've got to admit though; I'll be looking forward to tasting another one of Miss Cantrell's cakes. Mighty fine baker, that girl."

Seeing he would get no support from the two men, Trace excused himself. He strode off in the direction of the trail that led up to the rock formation the Bassetts called 'The Blowhole'. The massive natural shelf of sandstone sported a three-foot hole in the high overhanging roof. Legend was the Indians bore the hole in the rock ceiling to allow the smoke to escape the deeply curved three-sided room. Now abandoned, for hundreds of years the local Utes had used it for ceremonies and powwows. He could almost picture a crowd of Indians dressed in soft buckskin gathered around a large fire, listening to their chief tell them of days gone by.

Trace made his way to a low, hand-hued stone bench. Since discovering the spot, he'd come here often to be alone with his thoughts. He pulled off his hat and ran his hands through his hair. What was he going to do? He'd put everything in motion with the letter to Rock Springs and another to Denver. By dawn tomorrow, all hell would break loose. He hadn't been worried about the Bassetts. Old Herb had said they were intending to go over to the Davenports for their monthly Sunday services.

Now they were sure to still be around when the sun broke the crest of the eastern horizon. He didn't want them involved. They might turn a blind eye to the deeds of the outlaws that wandered in to take refuge in the bunkhouse, but they were good folk. And having J.J. and Miss Cantrell show up really put a wrench in things.

Trace looked down at his hands and remembered the tingle that coursed through them whenever he chanced to touch the pretty, raven-haired woman. A picture of her flashing, deep brown eyes and full, rose-tinted lips caused him to suck in a breath. What was the matter with him? She meant nothing to him. She was only a nuisance, nothing more. A muscle worked along his jaw and others tightened across his shoulders.

"Nobody's going to get in my way, not now, and certainly not you, Miss Cantrell," Trace announced to the smooth walls that surrounded him.

He stood to his full height and stared down at the thin trail of smoke that rose from the Bassett chimney. High bush and cottonwoods obscured the ranch house. He could make out the side of the barn and the corral. From this distance, he saw two men perched on the top rail cleaning their guns. It looked like Ketchum and Richards. A hard knot of hatred pressed down on his heart.

He would have to be extra vigilant. Nothing could happen that would tip his hand until he was ready and certain people were safely out of harm's way.

CHAPTER 10

It was turning toward dusk. The sky against the gray outline of the distant mountains displayed a blaze of pinks and oranges as the sun edged over the ridge. The spontaneous dinner party had been a success as far as the meal went. Chloe received compliments from everyone there on her chocolate cake.

Now the music started. Jasper tuned up his fiddle. Mr. Bassett joined him with his concertina, and Butch Cassidy pulled out a polished harmonica from his shirt pocket. One of the cowboys had rigged up a bass with a long pole and some horsehair string attached to an old dented washtub.

Chloe eyed each man in turn. For the past two hours, she had been listening closely for the name Harry. Maybe he wasn't here after all. Many of the men went by other names—Black Jack, Kid Curry, Flat Nose, Sundance, and The Tall Texan. Frustration and disappointment weighed on her shoulders as she gathered a pile of empty plates to carry back to the house.

Why couldn't Mr. Bassett have introduced each of them instead of just announcing her as their guest and them as 'The Wild Bunch'? She got a few doffed hats and bows of acknowledgement, but no one seemed too surprised at her name. In fact, the only unusual reaction had come from Trace Rawlings. He gave her a scowl and said, "little girls should stay at home where they belong," as he walked by.

Her blood boiled at the comment. Fists clenched, she turned to confront him, only to find him already halfway across the yard and taking long strides in the direction of the house. Why couldn't the man stand still for two seconds so she could give him a piece of her mind?

"I forgot something in the kitchen. I'll be right back," she said to Josie.

Josie smiled and put a hand on her hip. "I'll just bet you did."

Chloe gave her a look over her shoulder and marched toward the rambling building. What she would say to this outlaw cowboy ran through her mind as she stepped onto the porch and into the cool, dark interior. The fact that he wasn't in the kitchen or adjoining parlor pulled her up short. Where had the man gone? She'd seen him come into the house.

She stepped to a bedroom door as Trace came backing out.

"Oh, my!" she cried as her feet went out from under her and her backside hit the hard puncheon floor.

Momentarily stunned, she looked up to see Trace drop the chair he carried and extend his injured hand. "Oh, my gosh, I'm so sorry. I didn't see you there."

"Obviously." She ignored his offer of assistance and struggled unladylike to her feet, the swirl of her borrowed dress tangling around her legs.

"Are you okay?" He reached out to wipe dust off the long, periwinkle folds of her skirt.

Chloe stepped back. "I'm fine, no thanks to you. What are you doing in my room, anyway?" She looked at him with suspicion and pushed passed to grab the embroidered drawstring bag that hung from the bedpost. Pulling the satin ribbons apart, she gave a sigh of relief. The small 'carte de viste' still rested inside. The two-inch by four-inch photograph was her only clue to her half-brother. She hoped to show it to the right person tonight and have them recognize the woman and themselves as a small boy.

"What have you got there, a picture of your beau?" Trace asked as he stepped up behind her.

Chloe ran a finger over the serious face of her father. An ache of longing and grief caused her to catch her breath. It had only been four months, and she missed him as much now as the day he collapsed across his desk, dead of a heart attack.

~

Trace snatched the cardboard mounted photo from her hand. The sarcastic words died on his lips. The sepia-toned photograph showed a dark, handsome gentleman with heavy muttonchops and chin whiskers seated in an ornate tall-backed chair. Beside him, with one hand resting on his shoulder, stood a rather pretty blonde woman with sad eyes. Between the two adults stood a little boy about two-years-old. He favored his mother in looks and had a mischievous glint to his eyes.

Trace flipped the card over to see three names scrawled in faded ink. He handed the photo back. "Your family, I take it. Why aren't you in the picture?"

Chloe's hand jerked as her fingers touched his. She had to have felt the same jolt he did. Glad he hid his reaction better, he let her take the photograph from him and stepped back to give her space. Her head down, he could just see the hint of moisture in the corner of one eye. Good Lord, he hated to make women cry!

"Hey, I'm sorry, okay? It's none of my business." He reached for the forgotten chair and turned to leave.

"He's my father." She announced in a soft voice. "Was. I

lost him four months ago, but it seems like yesterday."

Trace set the chair down and leaned his good hand against the tall back. "I know what you mean. My folks were killed a couple of years ago, gunned down in their store for sixty dollars in cash. I think about them all the time." He pointed to the photo in her hand. "You don't look like your mother, but the little fella sure does."

"She's not my mother. My mother died when I was a little girl. I don't know who the woman in the photo is, but the little boy is my half-brother, Harry." Chloe slid the 'carte de viste' back in her reticule for safekeeping.

Trace watched her straighten her back and jut out her exquisite chin. Determination blazed in her dark eyes. "I'm here to find him."

Now that he was getting some useful information, he didn't want to spook her. "I'm sure you will, but this isn't exactly a metropolis. What brought you clear to the far corners of Colorado, Utah, and Wyoming? Seems like a pretty remote place to come looking for someone."

Chloe tried to pull herself up on the high bed. She gave up to lean against the hand carved bedpost. Trace worked to hide a smile. She was short enough, she'd have to hike up her skirts and climb if she really wanted up there.

She caught the grin. He sobered immediately.

"I'm not a little girl, you know. I'll be twenty-three years-old on my next birthday."

"I didn't say a thing." Trace spread his hands in innocence.

She put her hands on her hips. "You men are all the same. Even my father thought that just because I'm not tall and broad-shouldered, I can't take care of myself or run a business." She huffed and flounced passed him into the kitchen. "I can ride a horse, bake a cake, and probably shoot better than you, and I just finished my third year of college when my father died."

Trace straightened and put his hands up in surrender. "Whoa, there. I didn't mean to rile you. You suffragists carry this women's rights thing too far sometimes. It's just that, I don't think it's smart for any woman to be traveling in this part of the country by herself. Let alone one as young and pretty as you." He hadn't meant to say the last part. It just kind of slipped out.

He'd done it now. She was steaming. Her eyes flashed and her lovely, full lips firmed into a hard line. Her hands went back to her tiny waist and rested on the soft curve of her hips.

She's down-right beautiful when she's angry.

"Okay, Mr. Rawlings, I'll prove it to you. Give me your gun." She stuck out her hand.

"What! I'm not giving you my gun. You might accidentally shoot me, and I've already suffered enough at your hands." He held up the bandaged evidence.

Before he knew what she was doing, she had pulled his revolver from the holster cinched around his waist. The long-barreled gun looked enormous in her dainty hands.

"Hey, give that back. This isn't funny. That's a dangerous weapon."

Chloe ignored him and stepped out onto the covered porch. Off to the east, the music was in full swing. Josie was dancing with Sundance and Ann with Butch while the others clapped to the beat.

"See that rock sitting on that fencepost about twenty yards up the draw there? Watch."

Before Trace could react, she had the gun up and was sighting down the barrel. "This is a double-action Colt.38, most likely the 1892 model. You should try the newer Army M-model. It has a swing-out cylinder and better balance."

With that, she fired. The ping of the bullet hitting the

target and the rock flying from its perch confirmed her accuracy. Trace stood dumbfounded and slack-jawed.

"Hey, what's going on?" The music had stopped. Several of the cowboys were on their feet.

"Sorry, boys, I was just showing Mr. Rawlings here, how helpless I am." With that, Chloe handed him back the pistol, an impish, satisfied grin on her face. "It's pulling to the right a bit. You might want to have that checked out."

Trace pushed his hat back and scratched his head. "Well, I'll be…"

He watched her walk away, her skirts swaying with the swing of her hips. Trace looked back at the distant fencepost. Where in the world did a dainty little city girl—woman—learn to shoot like that, he wondered?

"She's pretty good, huh?"

Trace looked over at Josie Bassett as she came up to stand beside him with a plate of chocolate cake. She handed it to him. "Makes a really good cake, too."

CHAPTER 11

Trace and Josie stood off at a distance. "She thinks Harry may be her long, lost brother. Something about her father's will and wanting his company run by a man. I haven't had the heart to tell her that Sundance may be the Harry she's looking for." Josie crossed her arms and watched Chloe accept the hand of one of the men who'd asked her to dance. "She's a sweet woman, but I don't think she'd handle the news well."

Trace's jaw tensed as Matt Warner's arm went around Chloe's waist and they began to move with the music. "Yeah, well maybe she needs to learn the truth so she can go back east where she came from. Women like her have no business out here."

Josie reached out and smacked Trace's arm. "What do you mean 'women like her'? Yours truly is a woman, and I do just fine. So does Ann."

Trace looked down to see the fire flare up in Josie's eyes. "Whoa, now, I wasn't talking about you or Ann." He put his hands up in defense. "You two were raised here. I've seen you outride and out shoot a dozen men. I know you can handle yourselves." He looked up at Chloe. She had switched partners and was now in Sundance's arms, smiling up into his face.

"She's living in a dream. And the chances of it having a

happy ending are slim."

~

Chloe smiled up into his handsome face and tried to see her father's features there. His nose was similarly shaped, but that was about all. Maybe he favored his mother. The little boy in the photograph did.

"So tell me how you got a name like Sundance."

He smiled down at her through his mustache. "I worked on a ranch in Sundance, Wyoming, breaking horses. The cowpokes there started calling me that and I guess it stuck."

He wasn't much of a talker, but he was charming. Chloe would have her work cut out for her to get any information. "I saw you looking at Mr. Bassett's library earlier today. Do you like to read?"

"Best way I know of to escape and learn something new at the same time. Butch and I have that in common." He shrugged his broad shoulders. "I've always liked reading a good book. My ma was a stickler for reading and education."

Good, now we're getting somewhere.

"Tell me about her. What is she like? Where did you grow up?"

Sundance laughed. "You're sure full of questions, but if you must know, I'm from Pennsylvania. A little town you've probably never heard of."

Chloe's heart began to race. She needed to know more. Her mind filled with a dozen questions.

"Ma'am, the music stopped."

A blush crept up Chloe's neck and spread across her cheeks. "Oh, I guess I was more interested in what you were saying than the music." Her opportunity was slipping through her fingers. She had to think fast. "Mr. Sundance…"

"Just plain Sundance." He chuckled.

The blush deepened. “Right, Sundance. Could you help me for a minute? The cake is all gone, and I’m not sure everyone got a piece. It looks like we need to bring out my shoo fly pies.”

“Are you kidding? Shoo Fly pie was one of my mama’s specialties. I haven’t had it in years. Lead the way, my lady.” He gave a deep bow.

Trace gave her a scowl as she walked by. “Where are you two headed?”

Josie raised an eyebrow. “Maybe they need some alone time.” She grabbed his arm. “Come on, cowboy, dance with me.”

Chloe mouthed Josie a thank you and stepped up on the porch. Sundance held the screen door open.

“Thank you, sir.”

She needed to delay him long enough to ask a few more questions. “Mr. Bassett said I could borrow a couple of his books. Could you recommend a few to me since you know his library?”

“Sure.” Sundance walked across to stand in front of the far wall, where shelves on either side of the big stone fireplace stood crammed with books. “What kind of stories do you like?”

Chloe came to stand beside him. “Oh, I don’t have a preference. What kind of stories did your father read to you?”

Sundance visibly stiffened. “My father never read to us kids. I was the youngest of five, so he didn’t have much time for leisure. Just keeping food on the table occupied most of his time.”

This didn’t fit Chloe’s theory. *Maybe someone else raised him and the man doesn’t know the truth.*

“My father liked the Penny Dreadfuls, although he’d never admit it, being a successful businessman and a staunch

Presbyterian. He was a gun manufacturer, one of the best."

"Was?" Sundance turned and handed her a book.

"Yes, he died of a heart attack several months ago." Chloe took a deep breath. It was now or never. "That's why I'm here. I'm looking for my half-brother."

Trace stepped into the low-ceilinged room and let the screen door slam behind him. "Hope I'm not interrupting anything."

Why couldn't the man mind his own business, for goodness' sake! Perturbed, Chloe held up the book in her hands. "Sundance was just recommending some reading material."

Trace took the book out of her hand. "*Pride and Prejudice*, huh? Good story. I can empathize with poor, misunderstood Mr. Darcy." He quickly searched the shelves and pulled down another book. "Here, you might find this one interesting and enlightening."

Chloe took the thin leather-bound volume and read the title aloud. "*The Strange Case of Dr. Jekyll and Mr. Hyde* by Robert Lewis Stephenson. Sounds interesting."

"Yeah, it's about a lawyer who investigates a man who seems to have two opposing identities." Trace had a smug look on his face.

Chloe glanced from Trace to Sundance, who seemed to physically blanch at the comment. Realizing her opportunity to learn more about Sundance had vanished due to Trace's untimely arrival, she carried the two books to the kitchen table. "Well, if you two will carry out these pies, I'll just start cleaning up in here." With that, she turned her back on the men and began pumping water into the kettle to heat wash water.

"Yes, ma'am." Sundance picked up a pie from the sideboard and headed for the door.

"Take the other one, too. I need to have a word with Miss Cantrell about something," Trace said.

Chloe didn't look up as Sundance mumbled something and moved out the door. What could Trace possibly have to talk to her about?

He came to stand beside her. "You're barking up the wrong tree, lady. He's not your brother."

Chloe whirled on him. "What business is it of yours?" Her frustration bubbled to the surface. She was tired of all the uncertainty and mystery. "How would you know, anyway?"

Trace crossed his arms. Chloe noted how his muscles bunched under the tight sleeves of his light cotton shirt. With effort, she pulled her eyes away and looked up at his face. "I asked you a question, Mr. Rawlings." She lifted her chin and tried to put challenge into her voice. "How would you know Sundance's past—where he's from, and who his parents are?"

Trace pursed his lips. Was he buying time or deciding how much or what he'd tell her?

"I'm waiting." She tapped her foot for emphasis.

"Sundance is an outlaw, a thief, and a scoundrel. Why would you want him for a brother?"

Chloe huffed and arched an eyebrow. "Isn't that the pot calling the kettle black?"

It was Trace's turn to huff. "Lady, you don't know what you're talking about." He grabbed one shoulder and put the thumb of his injured hand under her chin. "These men are dangerous, me included. My advice is to climb back onto that buckboard and have J.J. drive you to the nearest train depot. You don't belong here."

Etiquette and propriety said she should jerk out of his grasp and slap him for touching her. She remained still. Would he pull her close and kiss her? Her pulsed quickened at the thought. What was wrong with her? What was it about this man—this stranger, that put her emotions all in a jumble and left her unable to think clearly?

~

Trace wanted to shake some sense into her. The touch of his thumb against her smooth skin caused other unwelcomed feelings to surface. Her head tipped back. Her eyes challenged him under a spray of dark lashes.

Chloe's lips parted to reveal even white teeth, and she smiled. "I can be dangerous, too. You saw me shoot. I'm just as good with a rifle. My father made sure of that. I can take care of myself, Mr. Rawlings." The smile disappeared. "Now, sir, unhand me or I'll scream. I don't think those dangerous men out there would hesitate to defend my honor."

This was not the time or place to stir up trouble with the others. Besides, Trace had been raised by godly parents to respect women. He took a deep breath and stepped back, dropping his hands to his sides. Shaken, he wondered if he was losing himself to this outlaw way of life.

"I'm sorry. I shouldn't have touched you, but I meant what I said. You need to get as far away from this place as you can before you get hurt." He held up his injured hand. "I might not be able to protect you next time."

He turned and walked out. The slam of the screen door punctuated his warning.

CHAPTER 12

Trace leaned against the tree and worked at the bandage wrapped around his gun hand. The cloth fell away to expose a bright red, blistered palm. Several of the puffy blisters traveled up his fingers, including his trigger finger. He grimaced as he worked the finger to loosen the stiffness that had developed. He could shoot with his left hand, but not with accuracy, and he was definitely not as quick on the draw. He re-wrapped his hand, only using half the bandage to give him more flexibility and still protect his palm. His fingers stayed exposed. *This could prove interesting.*

"Hey, Rawlings, you joining us?" Butch called out from the makeshift table. Four others had gathered to play poker. The rest lounged around the fire, picking their teeth and drinking. The ladies had retired for the evening. With Herb and J.J. entrenched in a game of chess in the parlor, the cowboys were free to play cards, cuss, chew, and drink hooch.

Trace much preferred a strategic game of chess, but he needed to keep an eye on the gang. "Yeah, just getting another lantern so I can see better to beat you hombres."

"Not tonight, my friend. I'm feeling lucky," Butch replied, leaning back in his chair with his hands behind his head.

"That's just the pie talking." Sundance reached out and

patted Butch's stomach.

Butch good-naturedly pushed his gut out and rubbed it. "That was some kind of dessert. Best shoo fly I've ever eaten and that chocolate cake was mighty fine, too."

"So is the baker. I'd make a cake with her anytime." Kid Curry snickered and made a crude gesture.

Trace's body tightened at the vulgar implication. Without thinking, he stepped up and kicked the chair out from under Curry, sending him sprawling.

A pistol immediately appeared in the outlaw's hand. "Big mistake, my friend."

Trace tensed, his bandaged hand poised to draw his weapon. *Now what have I done?*

He had never shot a man or been shot himself, and he didn't intend to start now. He eased his hand away and raised them both in surrender.

Butch dropped his chair back down on all four legs. "Ease up, Curry. Trace is right. You shouldn't talk about Miss Chloe that way. She's a lady, not one of Madam Fannie's girls."

"Come on, gents, let's play some cards," added Sundance.

Trace remained where he was, Curry's pistol still trained on him.

"Don't ever mess with me again, Rawlings. Understand?" Kid Curry holstered his gun and stood up. "Next time I might not control myself."

Trace let out the breath he'd been holding. Although there had been a time when he wanted nothing more than to see this killer dead, to have a shootout with him now, wasn't part of the plan. Neither was maybe getting innocent people killed. He needed a way to get the Bassetts, J.J., and Chloe away and he needed to do it before morning.

He handed Curry the gray ceramic jug of moonshine. It was a risky move. Harvey Logan, Curry's real name, got even meaner when he was drunk. The boys all knew he couldn't hold his liquor very well, and this stuff was a hundred and eighty proof.

"Peace offering?"

Curry hooked a thumb through the hole and swung the jug up to rest across his forearm. He took a long draw and wiped his mouth on his sleeve. "Whoo-hee, that sure has a kick." He bared his yellow teeth in a half smile and looked at Trace. "Say your prayers, cowboy, I'll be takin' all your money tonight."

Trace would be praying, but not about winning the pot.

~

Chloe watched from the window. The backdrop of firelight silhouetted the men at the makeshift table. Her body stiffened as Trace walked into view carrying a lantern. In the next instant, one of the men was on the ground pointing a gun up at him.

She put one hand to the glass and the other to her mouth. A gasp escaped her lips around her fingers. What was going on out there? Was Trace about to be shot?

Still dressed in the blue outfit Josie had loaned her for the evening, Chloe snatched up her shawl and raced from the room. *I have to stop this!*

She dashed passed the two old men hunched over their chessboard and out the door before they could stop her. Gathering her skirt, she raced across the dark yard toward the group of men. Her mind a whirl of images, Chloe didn't notice the gun was gone and its owner was now taking a long draw from a jug.

Trace turned. She caught the look of shock on his face and watched it turn to one of anger. "What are you doing out here? Get back inside where you belong."

Sundance stepped up to Chloe's side. "Hey, Trace, that's no way to talk to a lady." He turned to her. "But he's right, you really should go on back to the house." He cocked an elbow out. "Here, I'll escort you back." Over his shoulder he hollered, "Count me out of this hand, boys."

Confused by the quick change of events, Chloe looped her hand through his offered arm and smiled up at him. "I didn't mean to intrude. I thought there was going to be trouble, and I didn't want to see anyone get hurt," she said, speaking to Sundance, but looking at Trace.

The man scowled back at her. The lantern in his hand cast his features into evil shadows. "Remember what I said earlier, Miss Cantrell, this is no place for a lady." The warning given, he turned and joined the men at the table.

"How about you and I go for a stroll? It's a beautiful night and there's plenty of moonlight." Sundance smiled down at her. He quirked an eyebrow and crossed his heart with a finger. "I promise to be a perfect gentleman."

Chloe smiled up at the handsome, blue-eyed cowboy. He had the charm of her father, even if he didn't share his dark looks. "That sounds lovely. We can continue the conversation we were having earlier before Mr. Rawlings so rudely interrupted." She glanced back at Trace to make sure he heard. The look on his face confirmed he had.

"First, can I stop and get something in my room?" she asked.

"Sure, we've got all night." Sundance gave her a wink and turned toward the house, the big white mutt ambling along beside them.

"Seems you have another protector." Sundance nodded at the dog.

Chloe looked down at the shaggy animal. "Snow and Blacky, I don't mind. It's the two-legged kind that can be bothersome. Mr. Rawlings is of the mind that I should go home. That this is no place for a lady."

"He's a strange one, but then who am I to talk."

Chloe retrieved her bag from the bedpost and rejoin Sundance. Arm in arm, they strolled toward the corral. He released her hand and leaned against the log rail. "So what brought you out west, anyway?"

Now was the time. This was her opportunity to get the answers she'd been working so hard for. Chloe took a deep breath and held on to the second rail for support. "I came looking for my brother—my half-brother, Harry." She reached into her bag, pulled the small photograph out and handed it to him, then watched his face for a reaction.

Sundance's eyes opened wider, and he seemed to catch his breath. "Nice looking family." He cleared his throat. "So, what makes you think you'll find him out here?" Sundance gestured to the dark landscape around them.

It was time to tell the whole story. To give herself a minute to think, Chloe reached down to grab a handful of hay and held it out to Trace's red roan. The big gelding stepped up and lipped the offering into his mouth, then nudged her hand for more. She gave the velvety nose a pat and turned to Sundance.

"My father, Oliver Cantrell, met a woman named Anna back in Pennsylvania about thirty-three years ago. They had a son together—that's the boy in the picture. They named him Harry. Why they didn't stay together, I don't know, but my father never forgot his son. When he died, he left instructions for me to find him. Papers I found in my father's desk led me to Denver. I'm not completely sure about the last name. It could be Longbaugh, Longabaugh, or even just Long. A detective there suggested I try Rock Springs."

The words came out in a rush. Chloe took a deep breath and stilled herself to ask the one question that could change her world. "Are you my brother? Are you Harry?"

Sundance looked away from her and wiped a hand across his mouth. Turned away, she couldn't see his expression. Would he confirm her question or deny it? Her stomach twisted into a painful knot. Her hands suddenly became clammy and began to shake. She closed her eyes and said a quick prayer. *Lord, if he's the right one, please let him tell me the truth.*

A minute passed before Sundance twisted around, his back to the fence. He crossed his arms and looked off into the night. His face stilled, as if he'd come to a decision, and he took a deep breath.

"Not many people know my history, it's safer that way. So what I'm going to tell you goes no farther, understand?"

Chloe nodded her head and waited for his answer.

"My real name is Harry Alonzo Longabaugh. I was born in Mont Clare, Pennsylvania to Josiah Longabaugh & Anna Place Longabaugh. My mother was a devout woman. She would never have had an affair, of that I'm sure. Besides, she was too busy raising me, my two brothers and two sisters, and keeping my father happy." He paused, then looked down at Chloe with a half-smile on his face and sympathy in his eyes. "I'm not your brother, Miss Cantrell, and believe me, you wouldn't want me for one, anyway."

Chloe pushed off the fence. "That's not true. I'd accept you no matter what you've done or who you are. I was raised to believe in forgiveness and redemption. I forgave my father for his indiscretion the instant I learned of it, and I can do the same for you."

Sundance took her hand. "Chloe, I would be honored to have you as my sister. You're beautiful, brave, kind-hearted, and good with a gun." He chuckled. "But I'm not your brother. Even if I were, it's too late for me. There's a reward on my head and a warrant for my arrest." He sighed. "Maybe ten years ago I could have gone back to a normal life, but not now. I'm sorry. I hope you find him—the real Harry."

"But the photograph, you could be the boy. Let me bring a lantern so you can see it better." She moved to find a light.

Sundance put an arm out to stop her. "It wouldn't make any difference."

Chloe turned back to him. His expression one of resolve and regret. Her heart felt broken. Her hopes crushed. Disappointment mixed with relief that this handsome outlaw wasn't her long lost brother. *I could forgive him. I know I could, but the law won't. Even if he is my brother, he would never admit it, just to protect me.*

Chloe knew that in her heart this was true. Sundance could never be the brother she wanted and needed. The revelation settled into her spirit and quieted the hopes she had harbored. She forced a smile and reached up to pull his face down. On tiptoe, she gently kissed his cheek. "I wish you well, Harry. You'll be in my prayers every night."

Sundance gave her waist a squeeze. "Thank you. That means a lot. If I ever get back Pennsylvania way, I'll look you up."

Chloe stepped back and smiled up at him. "Try to stay out of trouble, okay?" She turned and walked away.

"Go home, Chloe. This isn't your world."

She didn't turn. Tears pooled in her eyes. Her heart told her he was kin, no matter what his lips said.

CHAPTER 13

His cards forgotten, Trace watched the two standing in the distance. The moon back lit their shapes as they came together. His jaw clenched, and his chest tightened as he saw Chloe's hands go up and pull the tall outlaw's face to hers. *What in the world was she doing?*

As if in answer to his unspoken question, Curry snickered. "Looks like Sundance has struck again. Seems like the little lady maybe ain't such a lady after all."

Before Trace knew what was happening, he had the front of Curry's shirt clutched in his good hand, pulling the man to his feet. The blisters bursting under the bandage, he raised his other hand in a fist.

In a flash, Butch wedged himself between the two. "Whoa, cowboy. Take it easy." He pushed Trace back and tugged his hand away from Curry's shirtfront.

Trace turned his focus on Butch. "You expect me to let him talk about her like that?"

Butch reached out and put his hand on Trace's raised fist. "No, it's just the liquor talking. What's with you, Rawlings? That's twice in one night you've jumped to her defense. You got feelings for the girl, just say so and we'll all back off. Right, Curry?"

Kid Curry Logan smoothed down his shirt and gave Trace a murderous look. "Yeah, right. But Rawlings, you touch me again, and you're a dead man."

Butch leaned into Trace's ear. "I suggest you take a walk, my friend, and stay away from Curry. Next time I might not be fast enough to stop him." He gave Trace's back a hard pat and turned back to the table. "Re-deal. Trace is out."

Trace couldn't head to the bunkhouse or he'd cross paths with Chloe, and he wasn't sure what he'd do or say after seeing her throw herself at Sundance. Instead, he turned toward the spring. He needed to cool off and clean up the ooze that now dampened the bandage on his hand. Tomorrow it would all be over. He'd be gone and with any luck, so would the gang. Chloe wouldn't have any reason to stick around Brown's Park anymore.

The thought cooled his anger and turned his focus on the morning's agenda. Nine months of hard work had gone into this, and now he needed everything to go as planned.

~

Chloe's eyes fluttered open enough to see the gray square of her window against the dark backdrop of the room she slept in. The evidence that it wasn't morning yet caused her to roll over and try to get back to sleep. The dreams of the long night had been relentless, leaving her exhausted and confused. Images of Trace and Sundance mingled with guns and shootouts, robbing her of any chance at a good night's sleep.

Quietly she dressed back into the functional dove gray shirtwaist she had arrived in yesterday. Her head hurt, so she decided not to pin up her hair. She brushed it out, leaving it to trail down her back in a drape of long, wavy, black tentacles. She grabbed her shawl and carried her boots to the bedroom door. The hinges gave a soft creak. She padded across to the outside door and eased it open. Two wet noses greeted her and tried pushing their way in.

"Shh. Everyone's asleep." She pushed the dogs out of the way and gently pulled the door closed.

Standing on the long porch in the chill pre-dawn air, Chloe wrapped her shawl around her shoulders and took in a deep breath. The sharp, clean smell of hay, sage, and pine announced it would be another beautiful summer day. The chatter of magpies and the low bellow of the cattle out in the meadow filled her with peace and calmed her spirit.

This is the day the Lord has made, and I will delight in it.

The verse made her smile. It was one of Aunt Clare's favorites. A sudden wave of homesickness washed over her and pulled the corners of her mouth down. She wanted to go home, to feel Aunt Clare's arms wrap around her and hold her against her ample breasts. Her quest to find the elusive Harry had worn her out, physically and emotionally. She's gotten her answer. She could go home now.

Chloe sat and worked her boots on, then stepped off the porch and headed to the outhouse. Within the hour, dawn would climb into the sky in a burst of glory. For now there was enough gray rimming the eastern hills to help her find her way down the worn path without a lantern. Blacky and Snow walked on either side like bodyguards. The two big dogs made her feel safer against the dangers of the night. Having to use the outhouse was her least favorite part of frontier life. The walk was bad enough, but the smell once she got there made her gag and hold her nose.

Stepping back out, she stopped to breathe in large gulps of fresh air when Blacky and Snow both alerted to something. Each gave a low growl and lowered their heads, their bodies stiff.

"What is it? What's out there?" Chloe bent down between

them and put a shaky hand on each hairy head. Could wolves or coyotes still be out hunting? The image of the cougar filled her vision. A sudden chill of fear made her tremble.

Please, God, whatever it is, make it go away.

Chloe calculated the distance to the safety of the big house. It would take her less than a minute if she ran as fast as she could. The bunkhouse was even farther away, so that was out of the question. She could hide back in the outhouse. The thought made her cringe and tightened the knot in her stomach.

A twig snapped. The dogs dashed forward and disappeared into the undergrowth, their growls and barks meant to intimidate any intruder.

"No, come back!" Chloe whispered.

Whatever she decided to do, she would have to move now or risk being caught in the open, alone and vulnerable.

CHAPTER 14

The rendezvous with the U.S. Marshals and two Pinkerton detectives went without a hitch. Trace filled them in on who was staying at the Bassett ranch. He drew out a diagram of the buildings on the sandy floor of the blow hole cave.

"That's the bunkhouse, and over here is the main house. I wasn't planning on anyone being there, but now we have two old men and three women to worry about. I can't really say how they'll react. If they think they're protecting their property and the women, the old men might take some potshots at us to scare us away."

Trace looked up at the men above him. "And don't be fooled, the women aren't helpless females. They're all crack shots. I'm not sure what Ann and Josie Bassett will do if they feel threatened. Those two know the Wild Bunch are all wanted men. They've gotten pretty close to a few of them. They may choose to protect them or try to escape with them." Trace thought about Chloe and the kiss he'd witnessed. "Miss Cantrell is an unknown quantity. She may have an interest in Sundance."

Trace stood to his feet. "No matter what, I don't want any of them hurt. They're decent people caught in a bad situation."

James Archer, head of the Denver office of the Pinkerton

Detective Agency, stepped up and put a hand on Trace's shoulder. "Tyler here has been working undercover as outlaw Trace Rawlings and been accepted by the gang. He knows these people, so take what he says as gospel." He reached into his vest pocket and pulled out a silver badge. "Here, I've been holding on to this long enough."

Trace took the badge and rubbed a finger across the engraved letters. "It'll be good to be an honest man again. Living this life has been harder than I thought it would be." He pinned the shield to his shirt. Finally shedding the guise of an outlaw felt liberating. He'd grown tired of all the lies and deception.

The oldest man in the group, a U.S. Marshal, cleared his throat and moved a wad of chew to the other side of his mouth. The soggy tobacco tinted the drooping sides of his handlebar mustache an ugly brown. "Mr. Rawlings, or I guess I should say Mr. Reynolds, is right. We don't want any civilian casualties." He broke open his rifle. Squinting one eye, he looked down the inside of the barrel. "Trace… gosh darn, I mean Tyler, I want you to cover the house. Make sure those people stay put."

Trace was about to protest when the man swung his hand up. "Now don't get ticked at me, son. You know you can't shoot with that hand. Besides, keeping those women safe is as important as bagging us some outlaws."

He spat a stream of nasty looking juice off to the side and snapped the Winchester closed. "Gentlemen, we're here to make arrests. I have the sheriff in Rock Springs getting the jail ready as we speak. Everyone Tyler mentioned earlier has a warrant out on them, but the most dangerous are Harvey 'Kid Curry' Logan, Black Jack Ketchum, and Ben Kilpatrick. They're known killers. That doesn't mean you let your guard down on Butch Cassidy, Sundance Kid or any of the others.

Those boys get cornered, they're liable to shoot their way out."

Over the next ten minutes, they worked out a plan. Guns loaded and checked, they drank down one last swig of coffee, and stamped out the small fire in the recesses of the cave. Trace worked his way back down the draw to the path leading to the main house. He heard the dogs barking before they came onto him.

"Quiet, you stupid mutts!" He admonished them as they came bounding out of the underbrush. The dogs romped around beside him, content to push their noses into his hand or the next rabbit hole they came across. At least they were quiet now.

He caught glimpses of the others moving into position along the ridge, shadows against an ever-lighting sky. A light-colored shirt flashed through the bushes as someone ran down the path from the outhouse. They looked like they were in a mighty hurry. Trace didn't like it. Something felt off. Had they waited too long? Was everyone waking up, ready to start another day? With six lawmen to nine outlaws, the element of surprise was crucial.

~

The dogs vanished into the brush.

"Blacky. Snow. Come," Chloe whispered. "Please, come back."

Fear awakened the adrenalin in her system. She needed to move, to get back to the house. With her skirts hiked up and head down, she charged down the path. Her feet felt mired in quicksand. A small cry escaped her lips as her heel caught on an exposed root and threatened to bring her down. She grabbed a handful of sage and managed to keep herself upright.

The glow of lamplight in the kitchen window beckoned her. *Thank God, someone was up!*

She burst into the room, the screen slamming closed behind her.

Ann dropped the kettle she was carrying to the stove. "Oh my gosh, girl, you scared the snot out of me. I didn't know you were up already."

Chloe registered the look of concerned on Ann's face. *I must look white as a ghost.*

Ann moved to pull her into a chair. "Sit before you fall down. What's wrong?"

"There's… there's something out there. I heard it. The dogs went after it."

In seconds, Ann was at one window and then another. Chloe watched her eyes searched the early morning landscape. Ann mumbled a curse under her breath and grabbed up the rifle by the door. "Wake everyone up. We've got unwanted company."

Before Chloe could ask who or what, Ann dashed out the door. Josie and her father staggered out of their bedrooms, Mr. Bassett pulling up his suspenders. His short, salt and pepper hair stood on end, haloing his skull.

Josie was tucking a plaid shirt into her breeches, ready for a day working the cattle. "What's going on? I heard the dogs barking."

Herb rubbed a hand over his head to smooth down his hair. "Sounds like cannon fire every time someone let's that screen slam."

Chloe came up on shaky legs and pointed to the window. "There's something out there. Ann saw it too. She took a rifle and went outside."

Josie moved to a window, her father to another. "There's movement on the ridge."

Chloe joined her friend. "There's someone moving along the side of the barn. What's going on?"

Before Josie or Mr. Bassett could answer, riders burst from the barn. Hunched low over their saddles, they thundered passed the house. Shots rang out. Chloe dropped to the floor.

CHAPTER 15

Trace crouched low and swung up onto the porch in time to see Ann run into the bunkhouse that joined the barn on the south side. He groaned in dismay. They needed the element of surprise if they wanted to avoid any gunplay. If Butch ran true to form, he'd already have horses saddled and ready in the barn, in case they needed to make a quick getaway.

An expletive popped into Trace's head. Before he could say it aloud, the double barn doors flew open. Horses, some without riders, exploded from the dark interior. Butch raced by, lying along the neck of his white mare. Sundance, Tom, and several others right behind him, riding low in the saddle.

Without thinking about his injured hand, Trace pulled his gun and fired off four shots as the horses and riders swept passed. Gun already out, Sam Ketchum fired back. Trace felt the burning sting of a bullet as it ripped into his thigh. He fell back against the log wall and sank to the floor. Pain, red-hot and lethal, gripped him as he pressed his bandaged palm into the hole and worked his belt off with the other hand. He gritted his teeth in agony. Blood pumped out around the wound.

Must have hit an artery. I've got to stop the bleeding.

The world tilted and turned black as he cinched the leather

belt tight.

~

Chloe covered her ears as the shots rang out. What was happening? Who was shooting? She looked up to see Josie move to the door.

"You can't go out there, someone's shooting at us!" she cried.

Josie looked back at her. "Trace has been hit. I need to bring him in. Stay on the floor. Pa, it looks like a posse trying to ambush the boys."

Josie was gone before what she said registered with Chloe. When Trace's name filtered through her panicked brain, she sprang into action and jumped to her feet.

I've got to get to him. I've got to help him.

Before she could get out the door, Herb Bassett grabbed her around the shoulders, his arms surprisingly strong for an old man. Chloe wrestled to break loose.

"Let me go, I need to help Trace," she demanded, then pleaded. "Please, he's hurt."

"I'll go, you stay here. Clear the table. Put some water on to boil and tear up a sheet to make bandages. Trace may not be the only one hurt." Herb shoved Chloe toward the kitchen. "Go, do as I say," he ordered in a firm, authoritative voice that brook no argument.

Chloe stumbled to the kitchen and retrieved the kettle off the floor where Ann had dropped it. Her hands shaking, she pumped water into the copper pot. From the window over the sink, she could see men running along the side of the barn and bunkhouse, guns firing. What was happening? Before her mind could register and untangle the scene before her, the door burst open and slammed against the wall. Herb Bassett backed in, his body bent forward under the weight of Trace's limp form. Josie followed, one of Trace's legs clutched under each arm.

All Chloe could see was blood. It was everywhere. His pant leg soaked in a deep, wet crimson. His shirtfront and Josie's were both splattered with the stuff. Chloe swept a hand across the trestle table, scattering a vase of wild flowers and sending a pepper grinder and a bowl of salt flying.

"Put him down here. Gently. Watch his leg." The amount of apparent blood loss and the chalky, gray tone of Trace's face gave Chloe new focus and banished the terror that had seized her.

Josie eased his damaged leg down. "He's lost a lot of blood, but he was smart enough to tourniquet his leg with his belt. The bullet's still in there. I'll have to dig it out and sew up the artery or he'll bleed out for sure."

Chloe looked up at Josie's grim face. "You know how to do that?"

Mr. Bassett turned from the stove where he stood pouring hot water into a tin basin. "Josie's ma was the only doctor we had after Doc Parsons died. My girl here was her mother's nurse from the time she hit fourteen or so. She's sewn up many a cowhand." He brought the basin to the table. "Don't worry. Trace is in good hands, but it wouldn't hurt none to say a prayer or two. The Almighty is the Great Physician after all."

Chloe tried to smile through her tears. The wisdom and calm of this sixty-ish man reminded her of her own father, who was always stalwart in a crisis. Thoughts of her father triggered a new worry.

"Where's Jasper?"

Although Herb Bassett's mouth was lost in the ruffle of mustache and beard, Chloe could read the concern in the man's eyes.

"He slept in the bunkhouse last night. Wanted to grab a hand of poker after we finished up our chess game."

Chloe gasped. "Oh, no! He could get caught in the gunfire!"

Before she could say more, a new volley of shots rang out. She ran to the window. Positioned along either side of the barn doors, a troop of strange men had their guns aimed at the dark mouth of the carnivorous building. Was Jasper trapped inside?

Her feelings for the old man had grown over the weeks until she thought of him as family. Family she didn't want to lose. She looked back at Trace's still form. Josie was using a knife to cut away his blood-soaked pant leg. His pale, chiseled jaw lay slack. His striking blue eyes hidden by a line of dark lashes. The tan of his cheeks now appeared as pale as his forehead, where his hat protected it from the sun.

She studied his chest for telltale signs of breathing. The movement of his lungs fighting for oxygen was barely perceptible. In a few short days, this man—this outlaw—had stirred emotions in her she didn't know what to do with.

His touch had been electric, like when she put her finger to the light socket of her father's desk lamp to see what would happen. The burst of energy that shot up her arm was strangely exhilarating, the power of the shock frightening.

Her feelings for this stranger were much like the experience she had with the lamp—exhilarating, frightening, and powerful.

She pressed a hand to her heart. *Is this what love feels like? But it was too soon, wasn't it?* Her questions would have to go unanswered for now. Trace needed her.

The gunfight went on. It seemed like an eternity to Chloe as she acted as Josie's nurse and assistant. The woman admonished her each time she jumped at the sound of gunfire.

"Chloe, you have to hold the skin back and keep your

hands out of my way so I can see."

"Sorry," was all Chloe could manage.

Without looking up, Josie asked, "Pa, what's going on out there? Do you see Ann?"

Herb turned from his station at the window. "No, only the men positioned in front of the barn. Must be sheriff's deputies or U.S. Marshals. I think I saw a flash from a badge on one of their chests. How's he doing?"

On top of the table and straddling Trace's long legs, Josie's arms were bloody to the elbows. Grim determination etched her pretty face. She didn't answer for a moment, then with a sigh of relief she sat back on her heels. "There, got it." She held up a smashed slug and tossed it toward the sink. "It nicked an artery, but I got it stitched up. His thighbone slowed the bullet down and kept it from traveling out the back of his leg." Josie's voice changed from triumphant to uncertain and wary. "He'll probably never walk right again, if gangrene doesn't kill him first."

Chloe swayed and groaned, her mind only hearing 'never walk and gangrene'. She collapsed on one of the long benches that ran down either side of the table.

Josie looked at her, concern on her face. "Whoa, girl, don't keel over on me now. Trace needs you to be strong."

Herb hustled out the door. "They're coming out. It's over."

Torn between her concern for Trace and her need to make sure Jasper and Ann were okay, Chloe stood. Josie must have read her mind and her intentions.

"Don't move. We're not done yet. Hand me that metal spoon. Be careful, the bowl is red hot. I need to cauterize a few places then I'll sew him up."

This woman's abilities and steady nerves amazed Chloe. Josephine Bassett was a true frontier woman—brave, strong, tenacious, and fearless. All the qualities Chloe felt like she herself lacked.

“You’re remarkable, you know that?”

Josie chuckled, looked over at Chloe for a second, and handed her back the hot spoon. “Honey, you’re pretty remarkable yourself. This is my life. I’m used to it. But you’re a city girl and yet you’ve managed pretty well out here in the wilderness. I’m impressed, and Trace will be too as soon as he hears what you did.”

Chloe looked down at the expressionless face. She gently patted a damp cloth across his forehead and ran her fingers through the thick auburn waves that fell back from his head. He needed a haircut.

She stifled a sob.

“Please, God, let him live.”

CHAPTER 16

"There, all done." Josie snipped the thread she'd used to sew him up. "As soon as the ruckus outside is all settled, I'll get some men to move him to one of the bedrooms. I'd say he needs to be in a hospital, but the trip would probably kill him. He's going to need a lot of care and attention for the next few weeks."

She went to the sink and pumped water into the basin. "Clean your hands real good, then his leg. Pour some of that whiskey on the incision and then tear up some bandages to wrap it with."

Chloe looked up in alarm. "But shouldn't you do that? I might hurt him."

Josie dried her hands on a large square of sackcloth and patted Chloe's shoulder. "You'll be just fine. I need to see what's going on outside."

Before she could protest, Josie was out the door.

Chloe set to work following the woman's orders. First, she gently cleaned the ugly incision, wiping the remnants of blood from his leg. She'd never seen this much of a man's leg before. She tried to concentrate on the task at hand. Even unconscious he had the ability to make her fingers tingle.

Pulling the top sheet off the feather bed she slept on only

hours ago, she quickly tore it into long strips. With tender care, she lifted Trace's leg and worked the makeshift bandage over his muscular thigh. With the lightest of touches, she placed her fingers over the stitches. "Dear Father God, please let your healing power flow through Trace's leg and bring him back to full strength."

The bandage securely in place, Chloe covered him with a patchwork quilt and eased a pillow under his head. Except for the blue tinge of his lips and his pallor, he looked like he was only sleeping. With his features relaxed and no worries of him catching her, she placed a hand along his unshaved jaw. In less than three days this man had ignited something inside her she couldn't ignore and wasn't sure she even wanted to try. On impulse, she bent to press her lips against his. "Get well, my love," she whispered.

Not wanting to leave Trace alone, Chloe stood in the open doorway and watched the scene unfolding in the yard. To her relief, Jasper and Ann stepped out of the bunkhouse, arm in arm. If it weren't for the grim looks on their faces, they might have been enjoying a Sunday stroll. Relief flooded her senses. She released a deep breath she hadn't realized she'd been holding. *Thank God, they're safe!*

Three men, arms raised, stepped from the shadow of the barn. Chloe recognized them as some of the men she'd eaten supper with the night before. Behind them, with a rifle at the ready, walked one of the lawmen. A second man had a hold of Kid Curry, clutching his own bloody arm. The Kid tried to jerk out of the man's grasp, only to stumble to the ground.

"Get up, Logan. You're not hurt that bad and I ain't going to carry your sorry butt."

Chloe couldn't hear what the prisoner grumbled back, but it must have been nasty. The marshal's face contorted in rage. The butt of his rifle came down across Curry's head, sending him sprawling.

Chloe cringed. She didn't like the man on the ground. He had a mean, callous way about him, but he didn't deserve to be struck when he was defenseless and wounded.

Ann ran over and pushed against the officer. "You didn't have to do that. He's wounded and obviously not going anywhere." Giving him a dirty look, she kneeled down and helped Curry to a sitting position. His arm forgotten, he used his good hand to hold the side of his head.

"Someday you'll pay for that, mister," Curry growled, murder in his eyes.

"You'll hang before that day comes, Kid." He motioned to another man leading a string of horses over. "Finish getting them saddled up and tell Murphy to bring our mounts. I want to be out of here in an hour."

All four prisoners were lined up along the fence, their hands tied around the top rail. "Hey, we gonna get something to eat before we go?" shouted one of them. The marshal wielding the rifle swung it to his shoulder and walked away.

Ann headed toward them with a bucket of water and a ladle.

"Stay away from them, miss."

Ann started to protest when the man swung around. "That's an order. Put the bucket down and join us in the house." He raised his gun and waved it in her direction. "I want to talk to all of you."

Jasper took the pail from her and put a finger to his lips. She huffed and scowled, but did what she was told and headed to the house.

Chloe backed up to stand by Trace's side as Josie, Mr. Bassett, Ann, and Jasper filed into the room while the marshal held the screen open.

Jasper and Josie came to the table where Trace lay

stretched out. Mr. Basset took a seat by the fireplace. Ann stood in the middle of the room, arms crossed and defiant.

Jasper laid a hand on Trace's arm. Concern deepened the crags that lined his face. "How is he?"

Josie lifted the quilt and examined his leg "You did a good job." She turned and looked from Jasper to the marshal. "He's got a pretty good size hole in his leg. Lost a lot of blood. If we can keep any infection from settling in, he'll make it, provided you don't cart him off to some stinking jail cell."

The marshal raised an eyebrow and addressed the room at large. "I'm U.S. Marshal Sam Bower. Two of the men out there guarding the prisoners are U.S. Marshals as well." He pointed to the two men standing near the door. "Mr. Williams and Mr. Archer, along with Mr. Reynolds here," he gestured to Trace, "are Pinkerton detectives."

Shock rippled around the room. Chloe was the first to put into words what they were all thinking. "You've got it wrong, Mr. Bower. This man's name is Trace Rawlings."

The short, barrel-chested man nearest to Chloe turned toward her and removed his hat as if he'd just realized it still perched on his head. He fingered the brim. "I'm James Archer, Tyler's boss." He nodded toward Trace. "His real name is Tyler Reynolds. He's been working undercover for almost a year now, trying to infiltrate the Wild Bunch. Did a mighty fine job of it too, I'd say. Shame Butch, Sundance, and the others got away, but we'll catch up with them soon enough."

Overwhelmed, Chloe shook her head. So much had happened in so short of time. Her mind couldn't quite sort and separate all of it, especially this new revelation.

The marshal pulled a folded pile of papers out of his shirt pocket and pressed them out on the table's edge at Trace's feet. "I have warrants here for each of the men tied to the fence out yonder. We'll be taking them back to Rock Springs to stand trial." He pulled a stub of pencil out of his vest and licked the end. "I'll need statements from each of you. Mr. Bassett, we'll start with you, sir."

Herbert Bassett looked up. His eyes behind the wire-rimmed glasses looked sad and defeated. To Chloe, the patriarch seemed to have aged considerably in the past hour. Would he and his family survive this calamity? Harboring fugitives was against the law, even out here in the Wild West. That much Chloe knew.

Mr. Bassett stood and worked his hands into his pockets. "Marshal, I'm a God-fearing man who stands on scripture and it tells me I'm to give hospitality to any who seek it, be he friend or foe." He reached down and fingered the cover of a well-worn Bible on the small table next to his chair. "It's not for me to judge, that's God's job and the job of men a lot smarter than me. That's all I got to say on the matter." With that, he sat back down, lean his head back and closed his eyes.

Chloe wondered how the man could be so calm after everything that had happened. Listening carefully to what everyone else had to say, she waited for the marshal to get to her.

Gray eyes finally turned her way, and the marshal's bushy eyebrows gathered in concern. "Miss, you look like you could use some air. Why don't we talk outside?"

Chloe started to protest.

"Go ahead, now that I've got some help we'll get Trace, I mean Tyler, settled in bed." Josie gave her a reassuring smile.

"They can't do nothing to you if you tell the truth," added Ann, who glared at the lawmen.

Chloe gave the two women a nervous smile and stepped through the door Mr. Bower held open for her. He was right. She needed some fresh air. Stepping to the edge of the porch, she looked off at the distant canyon walls the Green River passed through. Was that where Sundance headed? She wasn't sure if he had told her the truth or not about his mother and her father. She wished there'd been more time. She had a feeling she'd just lost something important.

"What will happen to them?" she asked without turning.

"We haul them back to Rock Springs for trial, but that's just a formality. They're all headed to prison or the end of a rope."

Chloe turned to the marshal. "No, I mean Sundance and Butch. Will you keep chasing them?"

The older man worked the brim of his hat than settled it back on his head. "Yes, ma'am. There are a lot of good men who've spent a considerable amount of time trying to catch them. They won't give up until those two are behind bars, along with the rest of the Wild Bunch."

"Men like Trace Rawlings—I mean Tyler Reynolds? Why does he do it? Turn himself into one of them, I mean?"

Now that the drama was over, questions crowded in, leaving Chloe restless for answers she wasn't sure she wanted to hear. She turned away and walked to the other end of the porch. "He isn't who I thought he was."

Mr. Archer stepped out of the doorway. "I can answer that better than the marshal here. Tyler Reynolds is a good man, misguided but decent just the same. He left his position at a thriving law firm back east to join Pinkertons after the murders of his parents. He wanted to get the men responsible and used us to do it. We knew what he was doing, but figured he had the incentive and drive to do whatever it took to be accepted into the gang."

"It's probably a good thing he got taken out of the action. I wouldn't want to be hauling him in for killing some outlaw before a judge has a chance to sentence him." Marshal Bower interjected. "Killing is killing in my book. Don't matter if one's a good guy and the other's a bad one."

Chloe looked at her hands. Gone were the soft, smooth hands of a debutant. Blood—Tyler's blood—had settled in around and under her ragged fingernails. Her chest tightened at the thought of him dying. She wasn't sure how she felt about the man now occupying the bed she'd slept in the night before. Was it possible to have such strong feelings in so short a time? And what about the deceit and lies? She'd imagined him as one thing—an uneducated outlaw lacking in scruples. In truth, he was just like her, running away from the grief of losing a loved one and trying to make things right.

Something in a crack along one of the floorboards glinted in the light and caught Chloe's attention. She stooped and worked it loose. It was a badge, the color of dull pewter with *The Pinkerton National Detective Agency* inscribed on its face.

"He must have dropped this." She held the shield up.

The detective walked over with his hand out. "I'll take that."

Chloe closed her fingers over it and dropped her hand into the folds of her dress. "If you don't mind, I'd like to be the one to give it back to him. You said yourself you were leaving and I'll be here looking after him." She didn't know where that last part came from, but she knew she wouldn't be leaving as long as Tyler needed her.

"Fine." He stepped back. "We still need your statement."

"There's nothing to tell. I'm only a visitor here. I woke up early and was coming back from the privy when I heard a noise so I ran back to the house, then all the shooting started."

Mr. Bower had his pencil poised above the folded wanted posters. "So you didn't know any of the men in these posters? Several of them are known to bring their girls along. You asked about Sundance, were you and he…" he hesitated, looking for an appropriate word.

"Romantically connected?" Chloe's chin came up. "No. I never met him before last night. He was nothing but a gentleman. Butch, too." Chloe stepped up to the marshal and crossed her arms. "Look, Mr. Bower, I've only known the Bassetts a short time and they may not see things the same as you or I might, but they're good people. This is hard country. It takes a lot to survive out here and you do what you have to do. Mr. Bassett gave those men shelter and food, just like he would give you if you showed up at his doorstep. You can't fault the man for living out the 'Golden Rule'." She reached for the screen door and pulled it open. "If I were you, I'd take my prisoners and be happy I caught the ones I did."

Her piece said, Chloe stepped inside and let the door close behind her.

CHAPTER 17

The ranch had grown quiet in the week since the lawmen had taken their prisoners and left. The marshal had warned Mr. Bassett that he better not hear of him or his kin interfering with the law in the future or it might not go so well next time. Ann had almost spit in the man's eye, except for her father's firm hand coming down on her shoulder.

"I'll keep that in mind, sir," the old man replied.

As soon as the posse and their captives rode out of sight, Ann headed to the barn, saddlebags riding one shoulder and a carpetbag in her hand.

"Where you going, daughter?" Herb asked.

"Best you don't know, Pa." She walked up to the chestnut mare Jasper had saddled and was tightening the cinch on. "Thanks." She gave his arm a squeeze. With determination, she secured the bags, then swung up into the saddle. She walked the horse back to where everyone else stood in the dirt yard. "I might not be back for a while so don't worry none."

Mr. Bassett moved to place a hand on her leg. "You're your mother's daughter through and through. Never could give up a fight, that woman, and you're just like her. But you're my daughter too, and I love you. Remember that and come home safe and sound, you hear?"

Ann bent down and gave the man a kiss on the top of his head. "I promise." She looked at Josie where she stood next to Chloe. "Take care of the old man for me, will ya?" Without waiting for a reply, she turned the horse and tapped her spurs into its sides. The dogs raced alongside her until she was out of sight around the finger of hillside that jutted out in the distance.

Chloe linked an arm with Josie's. "How long do you think she'll be gone?"

"Depends on Butch's plans." Josie smiled and patted Chloe's hand. "Come on, we have a patient to tend to."

Chloe's worst fears came to life late into the first night, when Tyler spiked a fever. His skin was hot to the touch, and his moans tore at her heart.

"Can't we do something?" she asked the others gathered around the bed.

Josie worked the bandage off the wound. A sour smell wafted through the small room. "It's infected for sure. I've done everything I can think of." She looked at her father and Jasper. "You got any ideas?"

"First thing in the morning I'll go gather some herbs Laughing Brook used to use and make up a poultice. Sage and pine tar are easy enough to find. Might take a little longer to get some aspen bark and schist crystals." Jasper's weathered hand patted Chloe's shoulder. "Then I'll head on over to John Jarvie's to see if the marshal sent word about a doctor."

"I'll go to John's. You get the herbs the ladies need," offered Mr. Bassett.

Chloe continued to bathe the sweat from Tyler's face and chest. Worry ate at her insides like a rabbit gnawing at his own leg to escape a trap.

He has to pull through. Please God, he has to.

~

Tyler was conscious of movement before he opened his eyes to see Chloe enter the room, carrying a basin. He kept them mere slits so she wouldn't notice he was awake and closed them when she turned to bend over him.

The soft breeze against his exposed skin when she pulled the quilt back and began bathing him with a damp cloth almost made him sigh. The lilac scent he remembered from their first meeting teased his nose. It took all he had not to react to her touch, but he wanted to savor the feel of her fingers against his skin.

It also gave him time to consider his options. He remembered getting shot. The pain in his leg gave plenty of evidence to the fact. What he didn't know was the final outcome of the planned ambush, or even how long he'd been out. As weak as he felt, he had a feeling it had been a while. He kept his eyes closed and allowed Chloe to bathe him, her touch soft and gentle.

"You really need to wake up. Please, Trace—I mean Tyler. It's been two days since your fever broke. Your leg doesn't look so angry red since I've been applying the poultices Jasper concocted."

She wiped the damp cloth across his forehead. "It's all over. The law is gone and so are Sundance and Butch." She stopped. Tyler heard water splashing. "Oh, Tyler, what were you thinking, risking your life like that?" There was a hint of desperation and fear in her voice.

"He wanted revenge. Simple as that." This voice belonged to Josie. "Mr. Archer told me, Tyler thought Kid Curry and Black Jack were responsible for robbing and killing his parents. They were using him to flush them out. Since half the gang got away, I guess the government boys will have to come up with another plan. So will our friend here if he's able to walk again."

Josie was right. Avenging his parent's deaths had been all he'd lived for since the awful day he found them. He knew the law, and he thought having the protection of a badge would justify him killing the men he was sure were responsible. Now a year of undercover work was wasted. Every time he had the opportunity to shoot one of them, he'd always managed to control the urge, knowing he might face murder charges himself.

A wrenching pain twisted in his gut. He couldn't stop the groan that escaped his lips. All he'd lived for and focused on for two years was destroyed. His parent's killers were free, and he was probably a cripple.

Chloe bent over him. He could tell it was her by the smell of lilac. "Shh. It's okay. You're safe here."

Safe? Ketchum and Curry surely knew who he was by now. Even if they didn't come after him, he didn't stand a chance of getting close again. Shooting them both during the ambush would have been defensible, within the limits of the law. He'd be doing the government's dirty work for them, ridding the country of desperate criminals, and that suited him just fine.

Thoughts of saddling Red and chasing after them filled his mind as he drifted back into the abyss.

CHAPTER 18

The afternoon light filtering into the room cast its rays across the prone figure on the bed. Chloe caught her breath. *He's looking at me!*

"You're awake." What a stupid thing to say. Obviously, he was awake. His eyes were open, and he was smiling at her. She'd worked out all the things she wanted to say to him during the long days and nights of combating his fever. Now, seeing his blue eyes staring back at her and that lopsided grin on his face, she forgot all the words. She stepped forward and settled into the chair beside his bed, afraid her legs wouldn't support her.

During the arduous hours of taking care of him, Chloe came to realize her feelings for him were genuine. The problem was she didn't know how he felt and there was the issue of his focus on revenge. She wasn't sure she could truly love someone who carried enough hate in their heart that they would scheme to kill another human being.

"What's wrong, you look like you've seen a ghost? I'm not dead, am I?" Tyler quipped.

Tongue-tied and flustered, Chloe stood and turned to leave. "I'll bring you some soup. You're probably hungry."

He grabbed her wrist and pulled her to a stop. "I'll let you go on one condition. You'll stay and talk to me when you come back. There's a lot I need to know."

Unable to trust herself to speak, she nodded her head and tugged her arm free. His touch still had the power to stir her blood and turn her into a kaleidoscope of contrasting and jumbled emotions.

She stepped out and closed the door behind her. Putting one hand over her heart and the other over her stomach, she took several deep breaths. It took a moment for her to realize she was being watched.

Herb Bassett sat in his rocker, an open book on his lap. "Has something changed? Is the patient worse?"

"No, as a matter of fact, he's awake and hungry." She gave him a quick smile and moved to the stove where she began ladling soup into a bowl. Josie had turned over most of the nursing and cooking duties to Chloe, since she still had a myriad of chores that needed doing each day.

"And asking questions, I would imagine. What are you going to tell him?"

Chloe placed the bowl on a tray with a glass of fresh milk and headed back to the bedroom. "The truth. At least what I know of it."

Mr. Bassett nodded his head and picked his Bible back up. "Good place to start."

She really needed more time, but Tyler needed some nourishment if he was going to recover fully. The sooner that happened, the sooner she'd feel free to head back home. The idea of leaving sent a wave of conflicting emotions coursing through her. She hated it here, didn't she? She missed home, Aunt Clare and Abel. She closed her eyes. *God, help me say the right words and make the right decisions.*

A grimace of pain crossed Tyler's features as he struggled to pull himself into a sitting position. Chloe worked a smile onto her own face as she set the tray on the dresser. "Let me help you."

"Thanks, I can manage. I'm not a complete invalid," he replied with a trace of sarcasm. "How long have I been out and helpless? And what about J.J., is he okay?"

"Jasper's fine. He's a little bent out of shape at you for lying to him all this time. He went off to his mine to stew, a few days ago." Chloe handed him a dishtowel to cover his bare chest. The thought of his deception distracted her, and without thinking, she set the tray across his lap.

He yelped out in pain, sending the tray and its contents flying.

"Oh, my goodness, I'm so sorry! I wasn't thinking!" she sputtered. The majority of the soup had landed down the front of her while the bowl did a wobbly dance at her feet next to the overturned tray.

"Geez, woman, what is it with you trying to kill me?" Trace growled.

Chloe couldn't stop the quiver that started in her chin and caused her lips to tremble. It was too much—the shooting, assisting Josie as she operated, the endless days and nights of watching him thrash and cry out in his delirium. Hurt, anger, remorse, and a dozen other feelings raged inside her. She clenched her hands into fists and flew from the room, bumping into Josie as she ran through the kitchen to the door. She had to get away before anyone saw her cry.

~

Tyler regretted the words the minute they left his mouth. What was it about this woman that always seemed to cause him to speak without thinking? As a law student, he'd been taught the importance of choosing his words wisely. In court, what you said could get someone hung or set a criminal loose.

"Chloe," he called after her retreating back. "I'm sorry," he muttered.

"You should be, you big oaf." Josie stepped into the room and gave his foot a slap. "What is it with you and her, anyway? You're like two cats in a small box taking swats at each other."

Tyler waved his bandaged hand, a frown on his face. "She… she…"

"She, what? That girl has been by your side day and night. She was up to her elbows in your blood, helping me stitch you up and save your life, Detective Reynolds."

Chagrined, he pulled the quilt up to cover his chest like a shield against her ire. "Everyone knows then." He had dreaded his friends learning the truth. Somehow, it was more comfortable having them think he was an outlaw.

"Yeah, your boss told us all about you working undercover for the Pinkerton Agency. I never could abide liars much or hypocrites." Josie stood there, feet spread and hands on her hips. "But the fact that you'd risk the lives of my family and friends is what really galls me."

Feeling cornered, he tried to shift the focus—another lawyer trick. "You weren't supposed to be here, and I sure wasn't expecting J.J. and Chloe. If you hadn't decided to have a shindig, none of this would have gone down the way it did."

Josie's mouth pulled down into a grim line. Her nostrils flared. She pointed a finger at him. "Don't you dare try blaming this on me or anyone else. This is all your doing, Mister Detective. Now Ann is gone. Jasper is gone. Chloe's worried herself sick over you, and all this stress has kicked up my father's asthma." She bent to pick up the tray.

Tyler thought she might hit him with it. Instead, she slammed the heavy ceramic bowl down on it.

"I don't blame you for doing your job. But hiding behind

the law to get revenge is pretty low. That doesn't make you any better than the outlaws you're chasing, in my book. At least Butch and Sundance aren't claiming to be something they're not." Josie turned to leave.

"Wait… before you go, let me explain." Tyler needed a chance to plead his case. He hated the idea that these people he'd come to care about, saw him in such a terrible light.

Josie didn't move. *Good, she's willing to listen at least.*

He leaned back and steeled himself to tell his story. "My parents were good Christian folk. Honest as the day is long. When I found them, there was a bloody trail where my father tried pulling himself across the floor to reach my mother. They died with their fingers entwined.

"I swore I'd avenge their deaths. I went home to Maryland and waited for a year for the law to do its job. Nothing happened.

"When I saw an advertisement that Pinkerton was looking for agents to work out of their western territory office in Denver, I thought it was an opportunity to gain inside information I didn't have. I quit the law practice I was working at and joined up.

"Almost a year ago, the opportunity came to go undercover. At first I saw it as a chance to put the men responsible behind bars, for justice to be served." He wiped a shaky hand across his face. "But something changed. I pieced together that Ketchum and Kid Curry were responsible for the killings. I wanted them to pay. I wanted them dead, but I didn't want to go to jail myself. I figured if I killed them trying to escape the law, I'd be justified."

Josie huffed and folded her arms. "Since when did killing someone ever become truly justified? You're going to be stuck in that bed for a while. I suggest you take a real hard look at yourself." Josie turned to leave and stopped at the door.

"You're a decent man, Tyler. You need to figure it out real soon 'cause I'm afraid Chloe is the one who'll be hurt the most if you don't."

Tyler had a lot of time to think after Josie brought him some more soup. He lay there the rest of the afternoon, examining himself. He didn't need a mirror to see he didn't much like what he saw.

She was right. He changed more than his name when he became Trace Rawlings. He'd let the need for revenge cloud the man his parents raised him to be. He'd allowed his values to become skewed in order to validate what he intended to do. It was time for a long, hard talk with God. Once that was done, he'd feel better about asking the people he cared about to forgive him—especially Chloe.

CHAPTER 19

Jasper tied the reins off and pulled his hat from his head to wipe his brow. It had been a long, hot, dusty ride. One neither one of them enjoyed making, Chloe especially.

Jasper turned to her. "You're sure about this, are you?"

"Yes, I've already said my goodbyes. Tyler Reynolds was right about one thing. I don't belong here. I didn't find what I came here looking for, so it's time for me to go home."

"Alrighty then." The arthritic old man made the slow climb down from the wagon and moved around to her side to help her from her high perch.

Once on the ground, she looked up into his rheumy eyes. He had become dear to her in a strangely parental way. She felt like she was sending him off into the world without being sure he could make it on his own.

With a hand alongside his grizzled cheek, she gazed at him through eyes quickly succumbing to the tears that had been threatening since the buckboard had pulled away from the dilapidated cabin. "Are you sure you're going to be all right without me?"

"I've lived nay on half a century without a woman to pamper me. Not that Laughing Brook ever did. Guess I can manage all right a few more. 'Sides you put that notice I gave you in the papers, I'm likely to have me another housekeeper before the fall. Course they won't be as pretty as you, but iffin' I'm lucky they'll know how to make a decent cake, and if they don't, I have your recipe to follow myself." He patted his shirt pocket and gave her a wink.

With a shy smile, he leaned in and kissed her on the forehead. "You take care of yourself, girlie. And I'd be obliged iffin' you'd let me know you got home safe and sound. Just send a message care of Jarvie's store."

She gave him an impulsive hug. "You take care of yourself, you old coot." Before her resolve crumbled, she turned and headed to the stone building to pay her fare. The weekly freight wagon stood at the riverside, ready to pull onto the ferry. It would carry them across the wide expanse of the Green River and was only waiting for her to climb aboard.

Good, she couldn't handle a long goodbye. *Better to make it clean and fast.*

Minutes into the trip, the driver gave up trying to start a conversation when he turned to see tears streaming down Chloe's face. She didn't care what the man thought; he was a stranger she'd never see again. The tears were for what she was leaving behind. If she were truly being honest with herself, it wasn't what—but who.

She hadn't gone back into Tyler's room after he accused her of trying to kill him. It was no good. He would never see her as anything more than a nuisance to be tolerated and looked after.

Within the hour, she'd packed her bag. She stood waiting while Mr. Bassett hitched up the wagon to drive her back to Jasper's place.

"You're running away, you know."

Chloe lowered her eyes and scuffed the toe of her boot in the dirt. "I know, but I don't see any reason for me to stay."

She looked up at the house. "He certainly doesn't want me here, and I need to keep looking for my brother. Besides, Father's manager only agreed to stay and run the business for six months. My time is running out."

Josie put an arm around Chloe's waist and walked with her toward the corral. "You know my mother would say some things are worth fighting for." She stopped and turned so they were facing each other. "But only you can decide what those things are, how far you're willing to go to get them and what you're willing to give up to keep them. That's the tricky part. I hope you both figure it out."

Chloe worked up a weak smile. "You've been a good friend. I wouldn't have made it out here in the wilderness without you." She gave the woman a long hug. "Could you do me a favor and don't tell Tyler I left or where I went? It would only muddle things up."

"My lips are sealed."

"And give him this for me, but wait a few days." Chloe handed Josie a small cloth-wrapped bundle. "It's a letter and his badge."

She turned to grasp the hand Mr. Bassett extended and pulled herself up. "I'm going to miss you, but I can't say I'll miss the Wild West. Keep an eye on Jasper. He's not as spry as he'd have people think."

Josie gave her a salute. "Will do. You take care. And write once in a while."

The wagon jerked forward as the horses leaned into their harnesses. Chloe held on with one hand and waved with the other. Turning forward, she took in the breathtaking vista before her. The red-hued cliffs marking the narrow canyon soared in the distance, God's touch of beauty in the high desert. Along with the people of Brown's Park, it was a picture she'd never forget.

CHAPTER 20

Tyler turned the tin badge over in his hand. With a frustrated groan, he threw it across the room and laid back against the pillows propped up behind him. A year of his life wasted, and for what? He hadn't been able to avenge his parents' murders, and now he'd likely have a gimpy leg that would keep him from going after their killers.

His hand came down to rest on the letter that accompanied the badge. Chloe's swirling script swept across the page to taunt him. He could almost see her trembling chin and the hurt in her eyes. She was gone, and it was his fault.

"Josie's right. Reynolds, you're an idiot," he said to his reflection in the bureau mirror on the far wall.

He was alone in the house and felt no compulsion to keep his thoughts to himself. His leg protested when he tried to pull it up into a more comfortable position. The single sheet of paper moved to the edge of the mattress and started to slide over the side. Tyler caught it and brought it up to his nose. The faint scent of lilac mingled with the ink. Or was it his imagination?

Her words weren't accusatory, but he could feel her disappointment and doubt. Looking back, he regretted some things he'd said as much as what he'd left unsaid. Now it was too late—she was gone.

Everyone around him—J.J., Mr. Bassett, and Josie, all expressed some level of unhappiness with him over his deception—especially J.J..

"Can't believe you thought you had to lie to me. I treated you like a son. Don't think I deserved that, you know." J.J. shook his head and released a wounded sigh.

"Plus, you chased Chloe away. You and that little lady have some unfinished business you best be taking care of once you're up and about. And I'd be thinking on how you're gonna move forward, 'cause, son, feeding on revenge and anger is likely to get you killed, and I'd hate to see that happen to you."

Those were the last words J.J. said to him five days ago. Herb Basset said pretty much the same thing. Only he added a few choice Bible scriptures and offered to pray with him whenever he felt the need.

With Chloe's departure, Josie became his nurse. She tended to his needs in silence most of the time, her displeasure evident in her face and her less than gentle bandage changing and bathing techniques.

That morning she came in with a tray of pancakes, eggs, and sausages. She set it down, none too gently, on the bedside table. "Best eat it while it's hot. I won't be waiting on you anymore, you're well enough to join us at the table."

Without another word, she left and returned with his extra set of clothes. "Chloe washed these up for you before she left. Your boots are at the end of the bed."

Tyler mumbled a thank you to her back as she marched out the door. With a shrug, he moved the tray to his lap. The sweet aroma of syrup and the tangy scent of spicy smokehouse pork moved his hunger up several notches. His mind shifted to the meal before him, and he dug into the pile of flapjacks with gusto.

Belly full, he gritted his teeth and worked his way to the edge of the high bed, glad his legs were long enough to touch the floor with room to spare. A picture of Chloe standing beside the bed, talking about her father, filled his vision. He looked at the neatly folded pile of clothes on the bureau. A sharp pang of regret at how he'd treated her sent a physical pain across his chest.

"She deserved better," he told his reflection.

"Yes, she did." Josie stood in the doorway, a set of homemade crutches in her hands. "You're going to need these. J.J. made them."

"Is he here?"

"No, he dropped them by yesterday. Said he didn't want to bother you."

"I would have liked to talk to him."

Josie leaned the crutches against the bed next to Tyler. "Don't think he's ready to talk to you right now. Pa's reading in the other room if you need help. I have chores to see to."

With that, she left. Tyler leaned over and pulled the clothes off the dresser. With a determined set to his jaw, he worked his legs into the clean pants and struggled to pull them up over his bandaged thigh. A firebrand of pain seared his leg as he put weight on it for the first time. He collapsed back against the bed and groaned in agony.

"I imagine you'll be hurting for a long while. Josie said your thighbone is what stopped that bullet. Here, let me help you." Herb moved into the room and reached out to support him. Together they managed to get his trousers on.

The effort was exhausting, but it felt good to be out of the confines of the small room and into the sunny kitchen.

"If you're willing, I could use a hand getting out to the privy, can't abide using that chamber pot."

Herb chuckled. “It doesn’t do much for a man’s dignity, that’s for sure.”

Back inside, Herb challenged Tyler to a game of chess. The two hunkered over the checkered board, strategizing and moving pieces around.

“You give much thought about what you’re going to do once you’re up and able?”

Tyler moved a rook. “That’s all I’ve thought about. That, and how much I need to apologize to all of you.”

“As far as I’m concerned, it’s over and forgotten.” He moved his queen across the board. “Checkmate.”

Tyler snorted and leaned back. “You’re too good for me.”

Herb reset the pieces. “Years of practice, my boy. I think of life much like a chess game. Follow the master plan, think ahead and execute your moves, then be prepared for the unexpected.”

The game momentarily forgotten, Herb leaned back in his chair and puffed on his pipe. “Never in my wildest dreams did I think I’d be living out here in the wilderness or raising five kids on my own. I was living in Norfolk, Virginia when I married my Eliza. She was a beauty, much younger than me, you know.” He smiled at the memory. “We had the world by the tail until my asthma got so bad it forced us to head west to a drier climate.” Herb sighed.

“Was heading for California when we landed here. Eliza fell in love with the place, so here we settled. God made her for this country. Best lady rancher there was. Then quite suddenly she died.” A sad frown pulled at his trembling lips. “That, I wasn’t prepared for. She was only thirty-two.”

He looked over at Tyler. “Life has a way of bringing a man to his knees sometimes, but I figure that’s the best way to talk to God. If you know him like you say you do, you might want to have yourself a conversation with him.”

Tyler bowed his head, not sure what to say.

Herb pulled himself up out of his chair and headed to the door. “I have some things to tend to in the barn. Josie’s out irrigating, so the place is yours.” He pointed a long, bony finger at the stone hearth. “You’re welcome to use my Bible. Got some good stuff in there. Might be useful.”

He settled his sweat-stained hat on his head and moved through the door.

Tyler sat there, staring at the abandoned chessboard. The old man was right. It was time to set things right, starting with himself and God.

CHAPTER 21

Now that Chloe decided not to return to college, her days were long and lonely. The girls she thought of as friends were all about shopping, engagement parties, and gossiping at afternoon teas. Home five weeks, she found it hard to adjust back into the life of Philadelphia society. She'd grown used to waking early and working all day.

While living in the city meant having the luxury of modern amenities, she now fully appreciated, she missed the fresh, clean air and wide-open spaces. A month-old letter from Josie had arrived that morning with little news.

Josie's father and brothers were well, although George got thrown from a horse and landed in a barbed wire fence, cutting himself up pretty good. They hadn't seen much of Jasper since she left. He seemed to spend more time out prospecting than he did at home these days.

Ann hadn't returned, but they got word she was with Butch in Utah. There had been a number of new train robberies across several states. Butch, Sundance, and the Wild Bunch were getting the blame for most of them, even though they couldn't possibly be in all the places reporting the heists.

Josie only included one line about Tyler. His infection almost gone, he was healing nicely.

Chloe looked at the single line of information and sighed. It said so little and yet so much. If he was on the mend, he could have easily written to her himself—if he wanted to.

She didn't understand her disappointment. The letter she left, along with his badge, pretty much wished him well, but washed her hands of him.

"It's time to move on," she told her reflection in the long, cheval mirror. With a resolve she didn't really feel, she pinned a hat in place and donned a pretty navy blue velvet cape and matching gloves.

Descending the wide staircase, she called for Abel.

"Yes, Miss Chloe," the short black man replied from his perch on a stepladder. The long white apron and the feather duster in his hand, evidence he was once again disobeying her orders.

She stopped on the bottom step and shook a finger at him. "I told you I'd do the dusting myself. Besides, I don't want you climbing on that rickety old ladder."

"But, Miss Chloe, there's no need for you to be bothering yourself with dusting and suchlike. Clare chased me out of the kitchen and I'm plum bored, to be honest with you."

"Well, I'll just have to put you to work, then. Could you please call a cab to take me to Father's office? And while I'm gone, I need you to pull a couple of rakes out of the garden shed. You can help me rake up leaves this afternoon."

"No problem, miss. I'll have a driver here in a jiffy."

Twenty minutes later, Chloe wished she hadn't made the trip.

Lucius stood near the window overlooking the Delaware River, a cocky grin on his face. "I think I've allowed you plenty of time. What, with your little misguided adventure out west, and the last month and a half since you've been back."

He moved across the office and came to place his hands on

Chloe's shoulders. She fought the urge to shrug them off and looked up at the man in front of her. He was handsome in a rakish sort of way. His hair, although thinning on top, was a rich chestnut brown color that complimented his green eyes. A European-style mustache covered his upper lip and accentuated the even whiteness of his teeth.

Chloe looked from the cleft in his chin to his eyes. She needed more time. "There's a proper period of mourning, you know. Etiquette says…"

He dropped his hands in frustration. "This etiquette nonsense, again. You want to know what I think?" He didn't wait for her answer. Instead, he paced the nicely appointed office. "I think you're manufacturing excuses. It's been six months since I asked you to marry me and I still don't have an answer, at least not one I'll accept."

Chloe rubbed a hand over her eyes and moved to her father's desk—Lucius' desk now. Where Oliver Cantrell was neat and meticulous, Lucius tended to spread his work out into disjointed piles. Chloe noticed several invoices with 'Past Due' stamped in bright red across their middles.

Papa would never have allowed the bills to get to that state. "Is there anything you need to tell me?" She nodded toward the evidence.

Lucius stomped to the desk and gathered the invoices. "Nothing you need to worry about." He shoved the papers into a desk drawer. "I have a meeting to attend, so if you'll excuse me."

He escorted her to the door and then blocked her exit. "I've made reservations for us tonight at Leon's. I'll pick you up at six sharp. Wear the sapphire satin. It's my favorite."

Chloe clenched her jaw, tempted to refuse him. She hated when he ordered her about like she had no say or opinion on the matter. Overbearing and bossy were not traits she appreciated.

She decided to be acquiescent to a point. “I’ll have to wear something else. That gown is being altered. Besides, its much too chilly out for something off the shoulder.”

His jaw stiffened. “Whatever. Just be ready. You know how I hate to be kept waiting.” He lifted her gloved hand to his lips and kissed it as he looked into her eyes. “Think about what I said. I’m anxious to make you my wife, Chloe.”

She smiled and squeezed his fingers. “I will, I promise.”

~

Lucius closed and locked the door behind her. He pulled an expensive pocket watch from his vest and clicked it open. Three o’clock, enough time to make it to the bank before it closed for the day. He gathered up his new leather satchel and worked his arms into a tailored wool overcoat. The handsome Inverness sported a short cape he felt gave him the air of a successful businessman.

Hailing a hansom cab, Lucius settled in and contemplated his future. He’d worked hard for Cantrell Firearms for nine years, moving up from the shipping office to supervisor and finally to plant manager two years ago. The idea of becoming the owner someday had never entered his mind until he realized Oliver might be old fashion enough to think a woman couldn’t run a successful business involving firearms.

That’s when he began his campaign to woo Chloe Cantrell. The fact that she was young and beautiful made the notion of marriage to the heiress very appealing. Although he held a measure of affection for the man, Oliver’s death couldn’t have come at a better time. Lucius needed an influx of money to keep him in the lifestyle he’d grown accustom to.

He smiled and leaned back against the high leather upholstery. This afternoon’s meeting would secure the funds needed to pay off his gambling debts and quiet his creditors. The smile faded as he thought of Chloe seeing the past due invoices on his desk. He would have to find a way of keeping her out of the office in the future. *Once she's my wife, I'll forbid her from showing up there unannounced.*

Forty-five minutes later, he came striding out of the bank, seething with indignant rage. *How dare they refuse him! The righteous little moneygrubbers.*

He ignored the waiting cab and stomped down the street, pushing his way along the crowded sidewalk for two blocks. Tossing a coin to a boy hawking papers on the corner, Lucius grabbed up the top copy of *The Philadelphia Inquirer* and scanned the headlines. In bold print, the banner announced the devastating fire that consumed the Reliance Storage Company and an adjacent building on Filbert Street. It went on to mention that seventy thousand dollars in damages would be paid out by the building owner's insurance company.

An idea began to formulate in his brain. The smile from earlier returned as he hailed a passing carriage.

CHAPTER 22

Tyler pulled the tan derby off his head and checked his reflection in the mullioned-glass of the ornate front door. His auburn hair trimmed, and the curls slicked down, he felt presentable. He ran a hand along his jaw, pleased with the smooth feel of the twenty-five-cent shave he bought that morning. Nervously, he tugged at his vest and adjusted the paisley tie at his throat. After months of soft cotton western shirts, bandanas, and canvas trousers, he found it difficult to return to the stiff collars and fashionable sack suits worn by Philly's gentlemen.

Satisfied with his appearance, he took a deep breath and tried to exhale his anxiety away. Would she invite him in or slam the door in his face? Either way, he had to see her one more time. He twisted the brass ringer and heard it brrrrring in the depths of the house.

A large black woman came to the door, wiping her hands on a white apron. "Can I help you?"

"You must be Clare Morrison. Chloe… I mean Miss Cantrell, mentioned you. Is she home?" He leaned on the cane that was now his constant companion.

Clare's eyebrows went up as she gave him a thorough up and down examination. "Who you be, young man?"

Tyler twirled the hat in his hand and tried to look confident and friendly. “I’m Tyler Reynolds, a friend of Chloe’s. Would she be available? I’ve come a long way, and it’s important I speak to her.”

The woman looked at him sideways and tapped a fat finger against her full lips. “So you be the one. Can’t recall she told me that name, but she did mention a Trace Rawlings.”

Tyler felt the pink creep up his neck. He wanted to run a finger under the stiff collar, but his hands were occupied. Had it suddenly tightened up on him? He had no idea what Chloe might have told the woman. He hoped she hadn’t cast him in too bad of a light.

Mrs. Morrison wasn’t giving an inch. With arms now crossed over her ample bosom, she eyed him one more time. “So you’re the cowboy what stole my girl’s heart. Came back here all pale and quiet, wouldn’t say nary a word to nobody. She threw herself into trying to run her pa’s company and fightin’ off the likes of Lucius Wheeler. That hasn’t worked out so well, so she’s been moping around here getting under foot. Now what you got planned ’cause I don’t want to see her hurt no more?”

Tyler looked around. Passersby were giving him and the formidable woman at the door curious glances. “Could we discuss this inside? I promise to be on my best behavior.” He put a hand over his heart and gave her his most winning smile.

The eyebrows rose once more while she considered his request. “Don’t have no gun on ya, do ya? I don’t abide no guns in my parlor.”

“No, ma’am.”

She stepped back and pulled the door open to reveal a marble-floored entry with a grand staircase to one side. “I probably shouldn’t be doing this, but I be curious what’s got my girl so prickly and serious since she came back from out west. I haven't seen a smile come natural to her face in weeks."

Conscious of his stiff limp, Tyler moved up the steps and into the foyer of the stately home. He looked around him, taking in the beautiful lines of the woodwork and the elegant furnishings. Although well designed, the place wasn't overdone or meant to impress. It had an air of comfort about it that reminded Tyler of his own boyhood home in Texas, just on a grander scale.

Clare interrupted his observations when she scurried passed him and headed to the back of the house at a quick trot. "Lordy, I forgot my pies!"

Tyler followed her into a bright, sunny kitchen that smelled heavenly. His mouth watered involuntarily with the aroma of apples and cinnamon as she pulled two tins from a carnivorous oven that dominated the room. Golden lattice criss-crossed the tops of the twin pastries and emitted a steamy waft of fruit and spices.

"Now I know where she got it from."

Clare set the pies on the wide windowsill to cool. "What you be talkin' about?"

"I've had your shoo fly pie and your chocolate cake. Chloe did you proud."

A wide smile spread across the woman's broad face, turning her eyes to mere slits. "She took to cookin' and bakin' real easy. Taught her everything I know. She'll make some man a right fine wife someday."

Tyler knew he'd won her over when she offered him a slice of warm pie and a glass of milk. They were sitting at the kitchen table talking about the death of Chloe's mother and father when a big yellow tabby wandered into the room and rubbed up against his leg.

He reached down and pulled the cat up on his lap. "And

who is this fella?"

"That's Magic, and he's a she."

Tyler turned to find Chloe standing in the doorway working navy blue gloves off her hands.

~

She couldn't believe he was here, sitting in her kitchen, holding her cat. Hadn't the man read her letter? When she left Brown's Park, she never thought or planned to see him again. As much as he was gone from her life, he still occupied most of her dreams—a problem she was working hard to remedy.

"I never expected to see you again, Mr. Reynolds, especially in my own house." She quirked an eyebrow at Clare.

The woman heaved herself up and headed for the kitchen door. "I believe I've got me some vegetables to gather for supper. I'll be out in the garden." At the door, she turned and gave them a mischievous grin. "You's in my kitchen, so I expect you two to play nice, ya' hear?"

Tyler looked from Clare to Chloe. "Yes, ma'am."

Chloe needed to stay in control of the situation and of her emotions. She lifted her chin and kept her eyes on the purring cat in his lap. *Traitor.*

"Why don't we go into the study, that is, if you're finished with your pie?" Without waiting for his answer, she turned and headed down the hall to her father's office. She hardly entered this room anymore—it was still too painful—but she liked the idea of having the expanse of her father's desk between her and this man who made her heart lurch just at the sight of him.

Sliding back the pocket doors, she took in a deep breath. A trace of Oliver Cantrell's pipe tobacco still lingered in the book-lined room. She hadn't had the heart to change anything in the masculine domain. His desk sat squarely in front of a bank of windows, his favorite leather chair positioned at an angle to the fireplace. Even his beloved hawkbill pipe and soft leather tobacco pouch still lay on the table next to the chair.

Please, Papa, help me be strong.

Chloe removed her cape and draped it over the high-backed office chair. She realized her mistake when the handsome leather and oak chair swallowed her up as she settled in behind the big mahogany desk. Feeling like a child playing grownup, she slid to the chair's edge and sat up as tall as she could, hoping the expanse between them would calm her frantic nerves and hide her trembling hands. She looked up as he limped stiff-legged into the room and moved to her father's reading chair. The last person to sit in that chair had been Lucius when he laid out his proposal of marriage and his plans for her father's company. The memory stiffened her spine and caused her to lift her chin a little higher.

Now she watched Tyler lean his cane against the hearth and slide the heavy Morris chair around to face her.

Chloe gasped as anger bubbled up. How dare he! What nerve!

"That's my father's chair," she informed him.

He sat down. A slight grimace crossed his face as he worked to cross his legs. He rubbed a hand along the wooden arm. "He had good taste. It's quite comfortable."

Chloe huffed. "What do you want, Mr. Reynolds?"

Tyler leaned forward, resting his elbows on his knees. His features took on a pensive quality. He sucked on his lower lip. "I came because of your letter."

He pulled a folded sheet of onionskin out of his coat pocket. Chloe recognized the cream-colored stationary from her traveling case. "You made a lot of assumptions in here, but you left before you gave me a chance to explain."

"I didn't need more lies. You were an imposter and you would have been a murderer if you hadn't gotten shot first." She shrugged her shoulders, trying to act like none of it mattered. "Sundance wasn't my brother. My search was at a dead end, so I came home. There was no reason for me to stay."

"And you think it was fair to judge me before hearing my side of the story? I'm a lawyer. I know all about damning evidence." He stood and moved to the fireplace, where he ran a hand through his auburn hair, causing waves to form where his fingers had been.

He's had it cut. Pity, I kind of liked it longer.

He pulled a gold pocket watch from his vest and clicked it open. "This was my father's. It was missing when I found their bodies. The robbers took it along with my mother's wedding ring and a locket that held the pictures of my sisters." He looked over at her with anguish in his eyes. "Do you have any idea what it's like to find your parents—people you loved—murdered in cold blood?"

Chloe blanched at the horrific image he conjured up. A nightmare no one should have to live through. She searched for words to express her sorrow for what he'd gone through. There were none.

"I'm sorry for your loss." It sounded so trite, but she couldn't think of anything else to say. She was about to ask how he got the watch back when he replied.

"I didn't tell you that to get your sympathy. I wanted you to have all the facts before you passed judgment on me." He stowed the watch away and came back to the chair.

Chloe noticed the marked limp in his steps and the tight line of his jaw. It had only been seven weeks since the shooting. Considering the damage done, he actually looked well and healthy again. A deep tan replaced the gray pallor she remembered.

CHAPTER 23

She watched him work his strong hands over the leather back of the chair he now stood behind. Another memory came to her of his hands on her shoulders. She let out a small breath and blinked.

"Well, aren't you going to say something?" he asked.

Chloe shook herself from her reverie. "I'm sorry," she stammered.

"You already said that. I need to know that you understand why I did what I did. I'm not trying to justify my actions anymore. I know I was wrong. It took me a while, but I figured that out. Your letter made me look at myself for who I had become." He paced the room with an uneven gait.

"I manipulated the law, something I abhor in other lawyers and swore I'd never do. I chose to sidestep God and took things into my own hands. If it hadn't been for your letter, I would have gone back after them as soon as I could walk again." He collapsed back in the chair. "Thank God, I didn't."

Chloe was lost. What was he talking about? She tried to remember everything she'd written in the note she scrawled before she ran from the Bassett ranch.

"I don't understand."

He lifted the tobacco pouch from the side table and pulled

out the book underneath. Her father's Bible. In all this time, she hadn't noticed it there. Since she refused to let Clare put any of his things away, it had sat covered up and out of sight.

"May I?" he asked.

Chloe could only nod her head, overcome with emotion at seeing the well-worn book. Of course, it would be next to his chair. She could picture him sitting there reading by the glow of the fire, thoughtfully puffing on his pipe. Tears pooled in her eyes. She dashed them away while Tyler leafed through the pages.

"You challenged me about taking the law into my own hands and doing God's job. I borrowed Mr. Bassett's Bible and looked up the verses you suggested I read." He cleared his throat.

"Recompense to no man evil for evil. Provide things honest in the sight of all men. If it be possible, as much as lieth in you, live peaceably with all men. Dearly beloved, avenge not yourselves, but rather give place unto wrath: for it is written, Vengeance is mine; I will repay, saith the Lord. Therefore if thine enemy hunger, feed him; if he thirst, give him drink: for in so doing thou shalt heap coals of fire on his head. Be not overcome of evil, but overcome evil with good. Romans 12:17-21."

He closed the Bible and put it back exactly where he found it. For a moment he didn't speak, his head bowed and his hands in his lap.

Chloe waited.

"Ketchum and Curry didn't murder my folks. Three weeks ago, I received a letter in the mail along with my father's watch and my mother's jewelry. It seems a couple of lowlifes—young kids really—heard Dad kept a safe full of money. When they found out that wasn't true, they tried to rob them of the cash in the register and the jewelry they were wearing. My father pulled his gun to scare them off. Instead, they ran out, firing behind them. They didn't even know they'd hit anyone until reading about it in the papers days later. Since then, they've been in hiding down in Mexico. A month ago they came back after hearing the Ketchum gang were being blamed. They got cocky and tried to pawn the jewelry right there in Austin. The broker recognized the watch. Long story short, they were arrested and are waiting to stand trial."

Still, Chloe remained silent, not sure what he expected her to say.

"I would have killed two men, maybe more, if it hadn't been for you. I would have become no better than them." He looked up at her. His eyes begged for understanding. "Mr. Bassett and I spent a lot of time talking while I recuperated. He helped me see how right you were and how messed up my thinking was."

"Herbert Bassett is a wise man. I'm glad you listened to him, but you didn't have to come all this way to tell me that." She cocked her head as a revelation came to her. He wasn't here just to apologize. Her heart began to beat a quick tattoo against her ribcage. Hope soared.

Tyler stood and came around the desk. He grabbed her hand and pulled her to her feet. "You're wrong. I had to come because I wanted you to know the whole truth. I couldn't stand the notion that you thought of me as an outlaw and a killer. Somewhere along the way, between rescuing you from that mountain lion and finding out you'd left, I realized your opinion of me was more important than anything else."

Her pounding heart stopped. Everything stopped. She looked from their hands to his face. His eyes searched hers, waiting for a response.

"What are you saying?"

"I'm saying... no, I'm asking you to give me another chance to show you who I truly am. For some inexplicable reason that's become very important to me. When you left, I realized *you* had become important to me. I haven't been able to get you out of my mind."

"Are you talking about Trace Rawlings or Tyler Reynolds?"

"I guess I never really got a chance to properly introduce myself." He bowed over her hand. "Tyler Joseph Reynolds, Esquire. Please to meet you, Chloe Elizabeth Cantrell."

The butterflies in Chloe's stomach soared. He had feelings for her! She sucked in her bottom lip and tried to keep the smile off her face. Fear, anticipation, and hope sparked a tiny flame in her heart.

~

All the misgivings and doubts vanished when she looked up at him. He pulled her into his arms. "Do you think you could give a reformed outlaw a second chance?"

The smile he thought he saw vanished. He watched hesitation flutter across her face, or was it fear? The battle going on in her head reflected in her dark eyes and the curve of her lips. She looked as frightened as the first time he'd laid eyes on her.

He released her and stepped back. "I'm sorry, I've overstepped my bounds." He moved awkwardly back to the chair and grabbed his hat, then reached for his cane. "I'll see myself out."

Without looking back at her, Tyler moved through the door and into the wide hall. He caught Clare eyeing him at the end near the kitchen. She pushed her bottom lip out and shook her head. He gave her a shrug and let himself out the front door.

His mind reeled at the lost possibilities. He hadn't thought much beyond seeing Chloe again. Pressure built up across his chest like a vise being turned as he stepped onto the sidewalk. He didn't have a plan other than to find a new job. Maybe his former law office would take him back. He'd given Pinkertons notice several days before. Wanting him to stay on, they offered him more money and a position in any of their offices across the country. He'd turned them down cold. No more outlaw hunting and impersonating for him.

He crossed the narrow cobblestone street and looked back at the stately red brick house. Chloe stood framed in the window, then the curtain fluttered back into place, and she was gone.

He took a deep, ragged breath and settled the derby back on his head. It was over before it had even really had a chance to start.

It's my fault.

Tyler swallowed the hard lump of pain and disappointment that threatened to choke him. He worked his finger under the stiff collar.

"Tyler."

He froze and closed his eyes for a second. Letting his hand drop, he turned around. Chloe stood on the bottom step, her hand gripping the iron rail.

She gazed at him with tears in her eyes. "Everyone deserves a second chance."

Chapter 24

The carriage Lucius hired pulled to a stop in front of the two-story colonial. He was about to climb out when the front door opened, and a man hurried out. He looked to be in his late twenties and well dressed. The silver-knobbed cane in his hand was more than a mere accessory. A pronounced limp forced him to rely on it to maneuver the stairs.

Instant suspicion made Lucius alert. When Chloe stepped through the door as well, he sat forward in the seat and watched through the window. She looked distraught and anxious as she called out to the man and said something he couldn't quite catch.

Lucius pushed the latch down and stepped out. "Chloe, is everything okay?"

She glanced at him and back to where the man hesitated on the sidewalk. "Lucius." She ran a hand across her forehead, seeming unsure what to do or say.

"Who is that man? What did he do to upset you so much?" He nodded in the direction of the stranger walking away and came to stand at her side.

"I'm… I'm not upset." She wrapped her arms around herself and turned back toward the door. "Let's go inside, shall we? It's getting nippy out here."

Lucius didn't miss the look of longing on her face as she stole a glance down the street. It was obvious the tall stranger meant something to her. But what? He escorted her into the house and closed the door firmly behind him.

Abel appeared to take his hat and coat. Lucius followed Chloe into the parlor. She walked over to the fireplace, where a small blaze burned.

"Chloe, I asked you a question. Who was that man?"

She kept her back to him, her hands extended toward the warmth of the fire. "Just an acquaintance. Someone I met in Colorado."

Suspicion still lingered, but Lucius decided to let it go for now. He moved to the brocade sofa and sat down. "I thought we'd have a glass of sherry before we left, but obviously you aren't ready. Have Abel bring me one while you change."

~

Chloe wanted to tell him she'd wear what she wanted, when she wanted. Instead, she silently walked to the arched entry as Abel came in carrying a silver tray with glasses and a crystal decanter on it.

"Miss, will you be joining Mr. Wheeler?"

"No, Abel, thank you. Please see to his needs while I change. And could you send Clare up to help me?"

Ever the proper butler when company was present, Abel gave her a slight bow and proceeded into the room. Chloe had to smile when she spied a couple of stray leaves stuck to his shoe and the back of his trousers.

The clock on the mantel chimed six times. Chloe knew without looking, Lucius would be drumming his fingers and counting each strike. The man was punctual to a fault.

She was slipping the green chiffon gown over her head when Clare came puffing into the room.

"Them stairs are going to be the death of me yet." She stopped with her hands knuckled on her broad hips. "So you sent the cowboy packing. Are you sure that's what you want, Missy?"

Chloe was untangling a strand of hair from one of the jet beads on the bodice. "No, I'm not sure at all." Frustrated, she stopped her struggle. "Could you help me, please?"

Together the two got her clothed and her hair done in record time. They stood at the cheval, Clare behind her with hands on her shoulders. "Go with your heart on this one, Missy. He loves you, I can tell." Their eyes met in the mirror.

"Who, Auntie?"

Clare turned her around and gave her a hug. "Your heart knows."

There was a soft tap on the door. Abel opened it a crack. "Excuse me, Missy, Mr. Wheeler is getting impatient. He doesn't want to lose his reservation."

Chloe gathered her skirts while Clare grabbed her cape and gloves. "Coming, Abel."

~

Lucius wasn't satisfied with Chloe's short, vague answers. She wasn't telling him something. *I'm going to find out what she's hiding.*

"How'd he get the limp?"

Chloe took a small bite of her cod. "Who?"

Lucius clenched his jaw. "Don't play dumb, it doesn't become you. I'm talking about the man I saw leaving your house today, and you know it."

Chloe shrugged her lovely shoulders. "He was shot in the leg."

He folded his linen napkin and laid it across his empty plate. "I take it you weren't the one doing the shooting."

The smirk and cocked eyebrow were meant to let her know he was teasing. Instead, she took offense.

"I most certainly was not. I'd never intentionally hurt someone." She wiped the corners of her mouth. "I believe I'm finished. I've suddenly lost my appetite."

The chin came up, a sure sign she was upset and going to be defensive. Lucius raised his hand and snapped his fingers. A waiter instantly appeared at his side.

"We'll each have a slice of the Cherries Jubilee and I'd like a brandy, please. Chloe, I presume you won't join me in an after dinner drink?"

Chloe smiled at the waiter. "Coffee for me, please, and only a small sliver of cake, thank you."

The waiter hurried away, giving Lucius the opportunity to continue his questioning. "He seemed rather despondent. Did you reject his advances?"

Chloe raised her chin a notch. "There were no advances on his part. He came to offer his apologies. I accepted. He left. That was all there was to it. Could we please drop the subject?"

The waiter returned. Chloe gave the young man a smile. "Thank you. It looks delicious."

Lucius ignored him and picked up his brandy snifter. "Let's talk about our engagement. I like that subject much better, anyway." He took a drink and set the goblet back down. "I'd like to announce it at the Harvest Ball. The best of Philadelphia society will be in attendance. That should allow you enough time to have a spectacular gown made. Who knows, we could make the society page if we play our cards right."

Chloe laid her fork down. "Lucius, I need more time. Why can't you be patient?"

"Because, I want you for my wife, *now*." He reached across and grabbed her hands. "You're everything I want in a wife—beautiful, smart, and stylish. If we married by Christmas, this time next year you could be presenting me with a son."

Chloe pulled her hands free and put them in her lap. "I'm sorry. It's such a big decision and I just can't make it right now. Please, give me time. I promise I'll have an answer for you soon."

Lucius wasn't happy. He had a timeline—a plan. Her reluctance to commit was making his life difficult, to say the least. He downed the remainder of his brandy and pushed his chair back.

"My patience is wearing rather thin. I'll give you one week. Seven days, understand? I love you, but if you can't appreciate that fact—or me—then I think I deserve to know one way or the other so I can get on with my life. You claim you would never intentionally hurt someone, but right now you're hurting me."

The speech got the expected result. Chloe looked contrite and chagrined. "You're right, I'm sorry. I'll give you my answer after church on Sunday."

Lucius relaxed. *This is more like it. I just have to be firm with her and pour on a little guilt. Better remember that for the future.*

He had no doubt what her answer would be.

CHAPTER 25

Chloe fidgeted all through the service. The worship didn't bring with it the normal calming effect she was used to, and the sermon failed to hold her interest. Lucius must have sensed her restlessness. He wrapped his hand around hers and leaned in to whisper in her ear.

"I can't wait for the service to be over. Reverend Samuels is awfully long-winded today."

"Shh, people will hear you." She looked around to see if anyone heard his comment. Everyone's face was turned to the front and seemed engrossed in the message. Chloe tried to relax. For her, the service was going by much too quickly.

I promised to give him an answer. What will I say?

She'd thought about little else all week, even making a list of pros and cons. It didn't help and only served to confuse her more. Her father thought Lucius was an excellent choice for a husband. At least she thought he did. He invited the man to the house often and trusted him to run his business. Even his will so much as said Chloe would have his blessing, if she chose to marry Lucius Wheeler.

She stole a look at the man beside her. He had a fine profile, straight nose, and strong jaw line. Although his lips were turned up in a slight smile, Chloe didn't see any joy in his eyes. Did she love him? She certainly cared about him. *Maybe I'll learn to love him once we're married.*

The service ended. Chloe linked her arm in his, and they made their way outside.

"I hid a picnic lunch under the church steps. It's such a beautiful day, I thought we'd walk over to Franklin Square and enjoy the fountain."

She smiled up at him, pleased by his thoughtfulness. She didn't want to give him an answer at home, or in the crowded atmosphere of a busy restaurant. *He really does have some good qualities.* The butterflies in her stomach settled down a bit.

"A picnic sounds like a wonderful idea. I'm glad I didn't tell Aunt Clare to expect us for lunch."

As they neared the big circular fountain, Chloe spied a man in the distance. He was tall and trim, wearing a derby and topcoat. The man walked with a limp. Was it Tyler? She hadn't seen him since that day at the house and assumed he'd gone back to Maryland or maybe Texas. Her breath quickened. She strained to get a glimpse of more than the man's back. He turned his face as he crossed the street, and her hopes deflated. It wasn't him.

"Chloe, is something wrong?" Lucius asked.

Her attention drawn back to the man beside her, she pulled her eyes away from the stranger and smiled back at him. "Just thought I saw someone I knew, but it wasn't them." She pointed to a spot under a large elm, its branches almost bare of foliage. "That looks like a pleasant spot. A carpet of gold and red just for us."

~

Lucius made a big deal of spreading the blanket out and setting up the food. Once everything was to his satisfaction, he took Chloe's hand and led her to the edge of the plaid oasis. He'd never been so nervous in his life and wanted everything perfect.

This wasn't how he'd planned it. A fancy restaurant and champagne would have been more to his tastes, but there was no money for that extravagance—at least not yet, anyway.

Chloe seemed pleased, if not a bit distracted. Lucius looked back at the figure in the distance. A wave of jealousy washed over him. *After today, she'll be mine, and soon everyone will know it.*

A leisurely lunch over, Lucius pulled out a small bottle of white wine and two glasses. "This is to celebrate with."

"But I haven't given you my answer."

Lucius popped the cork. "I'm thinking positive, my darling."

Chloe blushed. A sweet smile played on her lips. She cocked her head to one side. "That's the first time you've used an endearment. I like it."

"Well, you'd better get used to it. I plan to use them often from now on." Lucius grinned back and poured the glasses half full. "Before we toast, I need to hear your answer." He lounged back on his elbows, a glass in each hand.

He watched a play of emotions work across her face. She chewed her top lip and took a couple of deep breaths. It twisted something inside him to see her hesitation. Why couldn't she be excited and sure about marrying him?

He'd never had much love in his life. Oh, there'd been a few women, but no one of Chloe's caliber. She was everything he aspired to, and beautiful besides. He looked at the strands of black curls that framed her face and longed to pull the pins to let the rest fall in waves down her back.

When we're at home, I'll have her wear her hair down all the time.

She broke his reverie with a tentative smile. This was it. He held his breath and sat up.

"The first time you asked me, we were in a very public place, so I didn't expect you to get down on one knee there, but now it's just the two of us." She pulled her bottom lip in beneath a row of perfect white teeth.

Inside, Lucius stiffened. He hadn't followed the traditional route on purpose. To get on his knees reminded him of how his father had made him grovel whenever he asked for anything. To beg for the tiniest concession had been the only way to survive the harsh, overbearing man. When Lucius finally reached the point where he was as big as his father, the groveling stopped—only because Lucius left home—never to return.

Chloe waited, a look of anticipation on her face. Lucius took a deep breath and relaxed the grip he had on the glasses in his hands. He would do this once and never again.

"If that's what you want, darling, but you'd better enjoy it because it's not likely to happen again." While he nestled the glasses in the wicker basket so they wouldn't spill, Chloe stood up and smoothed her skirt, then worked the gloves off her hands.

Lucius moved to kneel in front of her and removed a small box from his pocket. Thankfully, the ring inside had been purchased long ago when he was flush with money. He was proud of the one-karat European cut diamond. A cluster of rubies and eighteen smaller single-cut diamonds in an Edwardian setting of rose gold surrounded it. The man he bought it from assured him it was worth a small fortune, and he was getting a deal since he wasn't going through a legitimate jeweler.

He opened the box and lifted it out for Chloe's inspection. "Chloe Elizabeth Cantrell, would you do me the honor of accepting this ring and marrying me?"

~

Chloe gasped at the size of the main diamond and the surrounding stones. *It's so big! What was he thinking?* The ring slid to one side. She looked from the ring to the expectant face before her. She knew he had his flaws and could be demanding and overbearing at times. He could also be thoughtful, considerate, and generous when it suited him. She loved how strong his hands felt when he helped her from the carriage and how proud he seemed of her when they were in public together.

The time had come. She couldn't put it off any longer. *Lord, please let this be the right decision.*

CHAPTER 26

Tyler looked up in time to see a giant man lumber toward him. The Goliath had to be six to seven inches taller than his own six feet. Everything about the man was oversize, from his log-like legs to his jug-handle ears, and sausage-sized fingers.

"Mr. Elliott, I presume." Tyler stood and watched his hand swallowed by Elliott's bear-size paw. He worried it would be crushed, but the squeeze was just enough to indicate the controlled strength of the man.

A wide, toothy grin split the visitor's face in two. "Mr. Reynolds. Good to finally meet you. Call me Andrew or Andy."

At the moment, he looked like a jolly giant, but Tyler could easily see how intimidating the man could be if he wanted. "And I'm Tyler, but I'm sure you already know that."

They settled at a table in the deserted dining room of the Bellevue Hotel where Tyler was staying. "I have to say, I'm intrigued by the telegram I received yesterday. Ernest Van Decamp didn't share many details, other than they need an investigator that isn't known in the Pennsylvania area—someone who would fit in with the local businessmen."

Andrew folded his massive hands on the white linen tablecloth and leaned in. "Mr. Pinkerton is looking for the right man to head up a new investigation centered here in Philadelphia. James Archer, from our Denver office, recommended you. Said you weren't interested in chasing outlaws anymore, but something a little more, shall we say—urban, might appeal to you."

The man had Tyler's attention when he mentioned the job was right there in Philly. His last conversation with Chloe had ended on a hopeful note when she indicated she'd give him a second chance. His hopes had instantly soared.

His funds were running low. If he wanted to stay in the city, he'd have to have an income. Out west, he could manage on very little, but here he needed a job. He planned to give himself a few days to check out local law firms in hopes of finding a position that would allow him to stay close to Chloe. His legal credentials and reputation were unknown this far north, and to Tyler's dismay, the bigger firms weren't showing much interest.

"I have to be honest with you. I'm not sure I really want to do the whole undercover thing again."

Andrew pulled a folded packet of papers from an inside pocket. "This would be a little different from the last time. No horses, no train robbers, and no using an alias. You'd be Tyler Reynolds, Attorney at law. We'd set you up in a small firm that handles injury law and property damages."

Andrew looked around and leaned in even closer before continuing in a low voice. "I've been working undercover myself for the past six months. Getting the goods on a loan shark named Johnny Blue. He's expanding into extortion and illegal gambling. I know how you feel about needing fresh, honest air to breathe. Existing on the dark side does something to a man's soul."

Tyler could see the Andrew meant what he said. Here was someone who understood the dangers of living so close to the sordid underbelly of society and how easy it was to let it overcome who you really were.

For the next hour, the two men discussed the details and made plans. By the time Tyler was back in his room that night, he'd met the two partners at Fletcher & Nolan and had a job as an associate in their law firm.

Byron Fletcher and Thomas Nolan were middle-aged bachelors, married to their practice. Neither one seemed to have much personality or the slightest sense of humor. Tyler found himself glad his employment there was only a cover for his real work—investigating a rash of fires resulting in huge insurance claims.

Working for the insurance companies and not necessarily the victims, his job would be to figure out if the claims resulted from negligence, accident, or arson and make his recommendation accordingly. Tyler planned to be fair and thorough, not picking sides and reserving judgment until each investigation was complete.

Before he could start work, he needed to secure a cheaper, more permanent place to live. The next morning, Andrew delivered him to a three-story Victorian, complete with a turret room on one side and a spacious wrap-around porch. Robins egg blue gingerbread trim and turned spindles competed with burnt orange shutters that framed each window and sat against the buttercup yellow clapboard siding. The whole thing looked like a giant, frilly Queen Ann dollhouse.

"You really expect me to live here?" Tyler asked as Andrew opened the wrought-iron gate.

"Miss Dolly is quite excited to have another man in the house. You'll be boarder number five. She only rents rooms out to professional, single men. I'm number three. She thinks I'm into security. My room is on the second floor. Yours is on the third floor, under the eaves. You'll have to share a bathroom with Mr. Smyth, but otherwise you'll have plenty of privacy."

"How much is this going to set me back?"

"Miss Dolly charges ten dollars a week, room and board. It's a great deal. She provides breakfast and supper every day and lunch on Sundays. She has a girl who'll do your laundry once a week for a pittance."

Tyler did a quick calculation in his head. The Bellevue was costing him three dollars a day and his meals were another three to four dollars every day if he ate well. Ten dollars a week compared to almost fifty made a lot more sense.

"I guess I can survive. Is the inside as frilly as the outside?"

Andrew chuckled. "You'll have to see for yourself, my man."

Suitcase in hand, Tyler followed the giant through the ornate front door and into a bright yellow entry hall that separated an equally yellow parlor and dining room.

"Did I forget to mention the lady is crazy about yellow?" Andrew whispered under his hand as a plump little woman descended the stairs, a vase of flowers in her hands.

"Why, Mr. Elliot, you didn't tell me your friend was so handsome." She almost seemed to bounce her way to them, setting the flowers on a lavish marble-topped table in passing. "How do you do, sir, I'm Mrs. Pritchard, but all my boarders call me Miss Dolly." She extended a pudgy hand for him to kiss.

Tyler gave Andrew a look over her head and worked a smile onto his face. "A pleasure to meet you, Miss Dolly." He leaned down and brushed his lips across the back of her hand. She gave a dainty titter and fluttered her eyelashes at him as he straightened back up.

Dolly Pritchard didn't seem to stop moving. Even when she was standing in one spot, she swayed and gestured with her hands. A cap of yellow curls danced around her face like golden springs set in motion by a breeze.

"I'm very picky about the caliber of gentlemen I accept into my home. A woman can never be too careful, you know. Andrew here tells me you're a lawyer. How exciting."

"Yes, I am. I'm brand new to Philadelphia and most grateful to find such wonderful accommodations."

"I do have a reputation for running the best boarding house in Philly." She batted her eyelashes at him. "That's because I treat my men—my boarders I should say—like family. My rules are pretty simple, and I'm sure you'll find them quite easy to follow."

She pulled a rolled-up sheet of paper tied up with a piece of yellow ribbon from her pocket and handed it to him. "I'll let Andrew here show you your room. Please join me in the parlor for tea when you're settled, and I'll have a receipt ready for you. You will be paying for a whole month, correct?"

"Yes, ma'am."

Just like that, Tyler settled into his new life, one he was eager to move forward with.

CHAPTER 27

Chloe played with the ring and thought about what she'd done. She hadn't told anyone of her engagement, especially Aunt Clare and Abel. Anxiety over what they'd say tinged the excitement she thought she felt. Clare would be vocal while Abel would give her one of his sad smiles that said so much.

"I should be happily anticipating my wedding. What's wrong with me?" she asked a porcelain doll sitting on the window seat beside her. Sylvie had been a gift from her mother on her third birthday. The last gift she received from her and something she'd never part with. Growing up an only child, Chloe had shared many secrets and sorrows with the pretty little doll.

She laid her head against the cold windowpane. "Am I doing the right thing?"

Lucius said he loved her. Still, something made her doubt his words. Did he really see her, or was she just part of a package? Marriage meant ownership of Cantrell Firearms would transfer to her husband. Was she as important to him as what she had? Uncertain of the answer, Chloe knew she had to learn the truth before she could fully commit to being Lucius' wife.

She needed answers, and the next morning afforded her the perfect opportunity. Lucius had mentioned he had a meeting in Reading with their main steel vendor. Since he would likely be gone most of the day, she would have ample time to look over the books in her father's office—now Lucius' office.

Gloves and cape on, hat in place, Chloe stood on the step, waiting while Abel hailed a cab. It was a glorious fall day, crisp air, piles of gold and orange leaves everywhere. She took in a deep breath, savoring her favorite time of year… well, one of them. She also adored spring when the promise of new things filled the air.

I think I'd like a spring wedding.

Chloe caught herself. Where had that come from? Yes, she was engaged, but was she actually considering a wedding? The thought chased itself around in her brain on the ride to the factory. A mile or so into the ride, she looked up in time to see a familiar figure moving down the sidewalk. Her heartbeat quickened.

"Tyler!" she whispered his name, sure it was him this time. *What's he still doing here?*

Without a second thought, she got the driver's attention and asked him to stop. He slowed the carriage and pulled to the curb. Before he could open the door, Chloe had it swung out and paused long enough for him to lower the steps.

"Please, wait. I'll just be a moment."

Tyler had disappeared into a nice looking brownstone sandwiched between two other similar buildings along a row of businesses. Chloe stopped in front and read the sign, *Fletcher & Nolan, Attorneys at Law*. Her curiosity working overtime, she stepped through the door to the tinkle of a bell.

Tyler turned at the sound, recognition and astonishment on his face.

"Chloe, what are you doing here?"

She tried to put on a confident smile and hid her shaking hands under the cape. "More to the point, what are you doing here? When you left, I assumed you were going back to Maryland or Texas."

He was wearing the same suit as he'd worn before, this time with a camel overcoat. He looked well, the cane more like a walking stick than a necessity. Chloe couldn't pull her eyes from his. What was it about this man that set her off kilter so much?

His smile reached his eyes and crinkled the corners into laugh lines. "I got a job here." He waved a hand around the room. "I'm the newest associate at Fletcher & Nolan."

Dumbstruck, Chloe's mind raced. He was here—in Philly—permanently. Her heart skipped a beat. "That's wonderful. I'm happy for you if that's what you want."

Tyler looked back at the secretary, watching and listening. He took a step closer. "After your last words the other day, I wanted to give us a second chance. What do you think?"

Her heart soared at the possibilities. Her engagement forgotten, she smiled up at him. "I think second chances are definitely in order. I'd like to get to know the real Tyler Reynolds."

An idea came to her. "Would you like to come with me to the factory, that is, if you can get away?"

"Although I do have an appointment today, I don't officially start until tomorrow. I stopped by to see if my furniture had arrived yet, so I can set up my office."

He turned back to the curious secretary. She quickly busied herself with the papers in front of her. "Miss Bateman, I'll be escorting Miss Cantrell to her father's factory, and hopefully, to lunch. If my furniture arrives, could you have it set up in my office? I trust you'll arrange it much better than I would."

The fiftyish-something woman smiled agreeably. "Of course, Mr. Reynolds, don't you worry about a thing. You and your girl have a nice time."

Your girl? Chloe liked the sound of that.

~

Pleasantly surprised at his good fortune, Tyler's spirits soared. He'd planned to contact Chloe as soon as he was settled, but it seemed the fates, or God, had other plans. He helped her into the carriage and sat across from her, their knees almost touching. She looked lovely, all bundled up against the chill fall air.

"I'm planning on making the rounds to the various businesses and manufacturers in the area to introduce myself. Guess Cantrell Firearms will be my first contact."

"I might be of some help there. I'm acquainted with all of my father's business associates. I was born and raised here, you know. What type of law will you be practicing?"

Tyler dreaded this part. He wouldn't outright lie to her, but there were certain things he wouldn't be able to reveal. "I'll be handling the property law side. With business booming here, Byron and Thomas can't keep up. It's mostly boring stuff—acquisitions, mergers, and representing business owners against insurance companies."

"That doesn't sound… well, okay, it does sound rather boring, but at least you won't be shot at, right?"

Tyler smiled at her. "Right."

Five minutes later, they pulled up in front of a large, three-story brick building, half a block long. The words *Cantrell Firearms World's Best Quality Weapons Since 1852* spread across the side in large black letters.

"This looks like quite an operation."

They stepped from the carriage and stood looking up at the massive building.

"It's grown a lot. Grandpa Joe, my Uncle Otis, and my father started it, but it wasn't until the War Between the States that they really began making a name for themselves. When Uncle Otis went to war and never came back, Grandpa just seemed to give up. He died not long after getting the news. Now that Papa's gone too, it's not the same. When I was a little girl, I used to love coming down here. I'd spend the day playing among the shipping crates and reading books under my father's desk."

Chloe touched Tyler's arm. He felt a rush of electricity even through the layers of cloth.

"Come. I'll show you around and introduce you to some of the men."

He followed her up the steps into the building, aware she kept her pace slow for his benefit.

They toured the factory floors first. Chloe greeted each man by name and asked about their families. It was obvious they all thought highly of her from their doffed caps and show of respect. Tyler watched her pick up a rifle barrel and roll it in her hands.

"The new bluing process looks wonderful, Jake. Keep up the good work." She smiled and patted the man's arm.

She's really quite remarkable.

Her father's office on the second floor became the last stop on their tour. Tyler noticed Chloe stepped into the fine-looking room with an almost reverent expectancy. A sad melancholy played across her face as she ran a hand along the edge of a handsome mahogany desk.

"My grandfather gave my father this desk when he turned the company over to him. It's older than I am." She turned back to Tyler with a sigh of resignation. "Now someone else sits behind it. I always assumed I'd run the company one day, but Father didn't think a woman had any business in the world of weaponry."

Tyler stepped close and laid a hand on Chloe's shoulder. "I'm sure he was only thinking of your best interest. This is a man's world, especially here." He swung his arm around to include the entire building. "Most people wouldn't consider this a suitable endeavor for a woman."

It was the wrong thing to say. Chloe instantly bristled. She glared up at him with a fierce expression on her face. "You would say that. You're just like all the rest. Keep the little woman in the kitchen where she belongs—making pies and babies." She lifted her chin, a sure sign she was angry and determined. "I know more about this business than any man alive, including Lucius Wheeler. If it weren't for my father's old-fashioned ideas, I'd be sitting behind this desk right now."

Tyler raised his hands in surrender. "Whoa there, Scrappy, I take it all back. I have no doubts you can do anything you set your mind to. But, you have to concede most people don't think the same way you do. Someday, maybe. After all, it's almost 1900. Who knows, a new century could open up a whole new world for women."

The clock on the wall behind them chimed the hour. The tour had taken longer than he expected. Tyler hated to leave her, but he needed to get his investigation underway. "I'm sorry. I have to cut this short. Like I said earlier, I don't officially start until tomorrow, but the owner of a building that burned down last week can only see me today."

"The Northrup Building. I've known Mitchell Northrup since I was a little girl. He's a hard man. Likes things his way and doesn't tolerate fools. You want my advice, don't try to be his friend, he won't appreciate it."

Tyler settled his hat on his head, loath to leave her still upset by what he'd said. "Would you meet me someplace for a late lunch?"

Chloe walked around behind the desk. "No, thank you. Lucius is gone for the day, and this may be my only chance to take a look at the books without him hovering over me in typical man-fashion."

Tyler played with the silver knob of his cane. "Look, Chloe, I'm sorry. I didn't mean to upset you. No one can question your intelligence or that you know this business inside and out. Truce, okay?"

Chloe pursed her lips, contemplating his apology. "So you think I'm scrappy, huh?" She smiled, a good sign she was over her burst of anger.

"Josie once said we were like two cats stuck in a small box taking swats at each other."

Chloe raised an eyebrow. "Guess you'd better be careful, Mr. Reynolds, you might get scratched."

CHAPTER 28

Lucius' meeting didn't go well. Reading Steel, their main steel supplier, was demanding full payment before they'd ship another order. Cantrell's supply was running low. If Lucius couldn't find a supplier soon, all production would have to stop. He didn't want to have to explain that to Chloe.

He spent the train ride back from Reading contemplating how he'd solve the problem. By the time he walked out of the Broad Street Station and hailed a cab, he had a plan.

"Take me to Blue's on twelfth."

Lucius leaned back against the leather-upholstered seat and pulled out his wallet. "Twenty-nine and change." *Not much of a bankroll.*

"I'll just have to make sure I win." He settled the expensive billfold back in his inside coat pocket.

The game lasted well into the afternoon. Lucius' pile of bills grew. He was ecstatic. *Just a few more hands.* Then his luck turned and his pile dwindled to nothing.

Excitement rose again as he looked at his cards. His muscles tensed with expectation. He laid out his hand. "Full house, kings high."

Johnny Blue chuckled and fanned his cards out before him. "Sorry, Lu. Guess it's my lucky day. A royal flush. Can't beat that." The man pulled the pile of money toward him.

Lucius gritted his teeth and breathed in and out of his nose to calm himself. This wasn't how he'd plan it. "Another hand."

Johnny sneered at him as he shuffled the bills into a neat stack. "Don't look like you're doing so well, Lu."

"You know I'm good for it. And don't call me Lu."

Johnny's blue eyes took on a look of cold steel. "What I know, Mr. Wheeler, is that you owe me six thousand, and word on the street is that you're into a few of my competitors for even more than that. That much debt can be unhealthy for a man."

Lucius could feel the sweat collecting under his stiff collar and across his forehead. He eyed the giant guarding the door, his bulging arms crossed over a massive chest. The man looked capable of snapping his neck without breaking a sweat or shredding a tear.

How'd I get myself in so deep?

The gambling had started when he was a teen throwing dice in the back alleys of the rough New York borough he grew up in. He advanced to cards and horses by the time he was in his mid-twenties. A big win meant living the high life, being noticed, and respected—something Lucius craved.

A long run of bad luck and the threat of broken legs drove Lucius out of New York and landed him in Philadelphia. It was there Oliver Cantrell met him when Lucius tried to sell him one of the new horseless carriages being produced for the Duryea Motor Wagon Company.

"I like your tenacity and spunk," Mr. Cantrell told him. "You should come work for me. I need more men like you. With your drive, you'll be in management in no time."

True to his word, Mr. Cantrell moved Lucius from the drudgery of working on the factory floor up through the ranks until he became the plant manager at the age of thirty-five. In all that time, he kept his compulsion for gambling a secret. In the past, he'd managed to cover his losses without too much difficulty, but lately a run of bad luck had piled on thousands of dollars in lost wagers.

Lucius eyed the big man again. He didn't like the odds of making it out of the room in one piece if he didn't win the next hand.

"You know, fellas, I think I'm done for the day." He pushed away from the table and nonchalantly worked his arms into his topcoat.

"What about my money?" Johnny also pushed away from the table and rested a hand on the pearl handle of a small derringer tucked into his waistband.

Lucius swallowed hard and managed a nervous grin. "Give me a couple of weeks, and I'll be paying everybody off with interest."

"So what, your favorite aunt die and leave you a pile of money?" asked one of the other players around the cigar protruding from the side of his mouth.

"Something like that." He turned to the door and came up against the human wall blocking it. "Johnny, you want to call your dog off."

Johnny nodded to the guard. "Two weeks, Wheeler."

The behemoth stepped aside and pulled the door open. Lucius jumped when the man snarled and growled at him as he moved through the opening. Laughter followed him down the hall.

He hurried to the relative safety of the street and hailed a cab, then realized he only had enough change for the trolley. Seething with indignation, he waved the driver on and ran to catch the red and yellow tram rumbling down the middle of the street.

It irked him to have to ride a public conveyance, something he hadn't done in at least five years. He grabbed a forgotten newspaper and hid behind it to hide his humiliation.

CHAPTER 29

Chloe settled in behind her father's desk. A comfortable feeling of familiarity surrounded her like a warm blanket on a frosty morning. Even though Lucius had left his own mark—the cluttered desktop being one of them—she felt her father in every part of the room.

Squaring her shoulders, and taking in a deep breath, she pulled the first jumbled stack of papers towards her. Squarely on top was a bill from their main steel supplier accompanied by a rather threatening letter. It stated that unless payment was made in full within thirty days, Reading Steel would be forced to take them to court. Until then, all deliveries would cease.

Chloe's heart raced. The breath she'd been holding rushed out, leaving her deflated. How could Lucius have let this happen? They needed the steel to make the barrels, frames, actions, and cylinders. Without this special gunmetal alloy, they had no business, which meant fifty-nine people would be out of jobs!

With shaking hands, she laid the bill aside and sifted quickly through the rest of the pile. To her dismay, it was more of the same. Red 'PAST DUE' notices screamed at her from the stack of papers. Chloe leaned back in the swivel office chair and took in, then let out several deep breaths. Was the company in trouble? Cantrell's had always been prosperous. What had changed? A headache crept in on her. She chose to ignore it and marched out of the office.

She found Lucius' new secretary busy typing away at the desk that had belonged to Agatha Collins for forty years. "Martha, please have Albert bring the books to my father's office immediately?"

The pretty young woman looked up at her in confusion. "I'm sorry, ma'am, but Albert doesn't work here anymore. He quit last week along with Mike Sweeney and Jack Mitchell."

Completely taken aback, Chloe moved past her to the hallway and into the bookkeeper's office. It was empty. The walls bare where Albert Sinclair's lovely seascapes used to hang. The visor and armbands he always wore hung from a spoke on the coat rack near the far wall. Chloe backed out of the room and moved to the stairs that overlooked the manufacturing floor. She hadn't noticed the change when she toured the factory with Tyler. Now she searched the faces of the men below, shocked so many familiar ones were missing.

Back in front of the secretary, she tried to keep her voice level and controlled. "Martha, please bring me the most current list of employees in every department?"

Before the woman could respond, Chloe disappeared into her father's office. She was working her arms into the sleeves of a blue duster when the redhead entered with the typed list.

"Here you go, Miss Cantrell. It's accurate up to last week. You'll see a red line through a couple of names. Mr. Wheeler let Harvey Matthews and John Stephens go last Friday. Is there anything else I can get you?"

Chloe's mind was in a whirl. What was going on? John was their master machinist. He'd been with the company for as long as Chloe could remember. She took the pages and tried to muster a smile.

"Thank you, Martha. I'll be out on the floor. It's almost lunchtime, why don't you go early."

"That's okay, Miss Cantrell. I eat at my desk when Mr. Wheeler's not here. He doesn't like the office left empty."

"Okay, would you send someone for me if Mr. Wheeler returns?" Chloe left the office and headed to the stairs. She climbed to the third-floor, planning to work from the top down. The large, open workspace smelled of wood and stain. This was her favorite area. She could sit and watch these craftsmen for hours as they shaped and designed the wood stocks and handles for the variety of weapons they manufactured.

She blew a relieved sigh when she spotted the curly mop of russet hair hiding the face of the man Chloe was looking for. Hard at work, Riley O'Connell concentrated on sanding a black walnut rifle stock. She came up behind him and cleared her throat. "I think you missed a spot."

The burly Irishman turned around, a look of surprise on his ruddy face. "Chloe, me lass, what a surprise!"

He wiped his hands on a rag and gathered her up in a bear hug. Setting her back on her feet, he looked her up and down. "My, but you've grown more bonny since I last laid me eyes on you."

Chloe giggled and twirled. "Not that you can tell in this awful duster, but I'm a young lady now. I'll be twenty-three next week."

"Twenty-three, is it? And I suppose you have a gaggle of young fellas chasin' your skirts."

"Well, I have had a proposal."

Riley instantly sobered. "Mr. Wheeler, I dare say." He raised a bushy eyebrow. "Watch that one, lassie. You can do better."

Chloe's smile disappeared. She worked the ring around to

her palm so he wouldn't see it and grabbed up one of the man's work-worn hands. "Riley, what's going on? I just found out about John, Harvey, and Albert Sinclair."

Riley gave a quick look around. When he seemed satisfied no one was paying attention, he led her to a quiet corner of the room and told her all he knew.

She heard a variation of the same story from others in each of the main work areas. Things had changed since her father died, and not for the better. Already the plant manager at the time, Lucius worked under her father's direction, but Riley and others said he changed when he stepped into the role as the Chief Operations Officer.

Lately, orders weren't being filled because of a lack of supplies, and the men hadn't been paid this month. Some of the newer ones had walked off the job when Albert announced payroll was delayed, and he couldn't give them an exact date they could expect their paychecks.

By late afternoon, Chloe left the building with knots in her stomach, while anger and fear did battle in her brain. Her next stop—the bank where her father was on a first name basis with the president. Stephen Phillips welcomed her into his impressive office and offered her a cup of tea.

"No, thank you, Mr. Phillips. This isn't a social visit, I'm afraid. I need to know the financial status of Cantrell Firearms. It's recently come to my attention that there might be some problems, and I'd like to see what I can do to solve them."

The distinguished, gray-haired banker cleared his throat and folded his hands on his desk blotter. "Miss Cantrell, I understand your concerns, but I'm afraid I'm not at liberty to discuss the financial issues your father's company is currently facing."

Chloe moved to the edge of her chair and straightened her back. "I may not run the company, but I am my father's only heir. I'll do everything in my power to see that his legacy and reputation remains untainted."

"That's admirable. I wouldn't expect anything less from a daughter of Oliver Cantrell. However, this might be a conversation best had with Mr. Wheeler and your father's attorney. I have to honor the confidentiality clause the bank has with your father's company."

Chloe could tell she would get nowhere with the man. "Okay, but I understand the workers haven't been paid this month." She pulled a sheet of paper out of her bag and slid it across the desk. "Here's the list of men and what each is owed. If I put funds into the payroll account, could you see that each of these men gets what is due him? You can add compensation for the bank's time, of course."

Mr. Phillips looked at the list and ran a finger down the column of figures to the bottom. "This is quite a large sum. May I ask how you propose to cover it?"

"If you agree to handle this for me, I would like to transfer the necessary funds from my trust."

The banker looked at her in surprise. "Are you sure you want to do that? What will you do if this should happen next month, or the month after that? I understand there are several creditors who are also demanding payment. Do you intend to cover those costs, too?"

Chloe's chin came up. "I assure you, Mr. Phillips, my father would never allow this to happen, and I don't intend to either." She rose and clutched her purse. With her back ramrod straight, she asked. "Can you help me with this or not, sir?"

The bank president hesitated, then rose and nodded his head. "I'll take care of it this time. But, Miss Cantrell, I'd advise you to speak to your father's attorney, and perhaps it might be in your best interest to engage one for yourself."

Chloe left the impressive building a wreck. Her mind and emotions in chaos. She needed to confront Lucius, and she needed to do it soon. The thought caused her stomach to churn with dread.

CHAPTER 30

Tyler pushed away from his desk and stretched. It was almost eight. Time to call it a day. He rubbed a hand up and down his leg to ease the cramping that seemed to be his constant companion.

His first couple of days on the job had been busy with a handful of client files to review. All were claims being fought by insurance companies. Of the six, four were worth investigating as possible arson caused by the owners, extortionists, or some other unknown parties. Two were victims trying to collect on—what he felt—were legitimate claims the insurance companies were fighting.

He spent his time interviewing the various litigants, as well as touring the properties in question. All were businesses, ranging from a small grocer to a huge clothing manufacturer. Tyler spoke with the fire investigator and learned more than he ever wanted to know about how fires started by accident or when set intentionally.

Tired, his eyes blurry from reading documents, Tyler shrugged into his coat and grabbed up his cane and hat. The weather had turned cold and blustery. Not a good night to walk the six blocks to his new home at Miss Dolly's.

He stepped outside and caught a trolley that would take

him within a block of Chloe's house, eager to see her again after their impromptu tour of her father's building.

Tyler climbed the steps to her front door and rang the bell. Anticipation at seeing her again began to build. When he heard someone moving to open the door, he pulled his hat from his head. The dark face of an older gentleman, dressed in butler's livery, looked around the edge of the doorframe.

"May I help you, sir?"

"You must be Abel, Clare's husband." Tyler displayed his most winning smile.

Surprised, Abel opened the door the rest of the way. "Yes, sir, I'm Mr. Morrison."

"You're one lucky man. Clare sure knows her way around a pie." Tyler stuck his hand out. "I'm Tyler Reynolds, Mr. Morrison."

Abel shook his hand with a rather confused look on his face. Before anything else could be said, Clare appeared wiping her hands on the expansive white apron that covered the front of her.

"Abel, who's at the door at this hour? We weren't expecting company."

Tyler stepped into her view. "It's me, Miss Clare. Sorry I didn't call first. I was hoping to catch Chloe at home. I'd like to take her to supper."

A wide smile spread across the woman's face and turned her eyes to slits. "Mr. Tyler, come in, come in." She linked an arm in his and drew him into the parlor. "I'm afraid Miss Chloe's not here. She's been gone 'til all hours the past couple of nights. That Lucius Wheeler has been looking for her, too."

Tyler came to a stop by the fireplace and extended his hands to its warmth. He turned in time to catch a look pass between husband and wife.

"Oh shush, Abel." She waved a corner of her apron at the

man. “Mr. Tyler here is a close friend of Miss Chloe’s from Colorado. The one I told you about.” She wiggled an eyebrow. “I reckon he’d want to know if something’s going on with our girl. Right, Mr. Tyler?”

A thread of concern tightened around Tyler’s heart. “Is there a problem?”

Raised eyebrows between the pair, and a frown on Abel’s face deepened his concern. Something was going on, and it had to do with Chloe. “Abel, I assure you, I only want the best for Chloe. I’ll do everything in my power to protect her, but I need to know what you know.”

Another wave of unspoken communication passed between the pair.

“Please, I want to help.”

“Come sit down. We’ll tell you what we know, which ain’t much,” she said.

Clare settled her ample body on to a delicate settee and pulled Abel down beside her. Tyler took a seat across from them.

“First, let me start by saying I don’t normally share Miss Chloe’s business with outsiders, but we’re worried about her, aren’t we, Abel?” Clare gathered her husband’s hand into hers. “Chloe came home two days ago looking like a ghost, all pale and shaky. I thought she was coming down with something and hustled her off to bed with a bowl of my chicken and dumpling soup. She barely touched it and hasn’t eaten hardly a thing since.”

“That’s not the important part,” Abel interrupted. “She made a bunch of telephone calls first thing the next morning, then had me arrange a carriage and driver for the whole day. Did the same thing again this morning.”

“She left here looking like a strong wind could blow her over, all pinch-faced. I could tell she’d been crying. Wouldn’t tell me a thing when I asked what was wrong, just told me not to worry." Clare huffed and shook her head. "Our girl's in trouble, I can feel it in my bones."

Tyler left a few minutes later, promising he'd find Chloe and get to the bottom of whatever was going on with her. He sat on the hard tram seat and tried to rub the tension out of his neck.

His mind riled with possible scenarios. *What have you gotten yourself into this time, Chloe Cantrell?*

CHAPTER 31

Chloe felt along the wall for the switch. She would have rather felt her way in the dark, but the long flight of stairs to the cluster of offices could be treacherous. One dim bulb tried but failed to properly illuminate the angled staircase. At the top, she tiptoed down the hall and eased the door open to the outer office.

The sun had long set, and now a beam of moonlight filtered through the window. No one occupied the room—not that she expected Martha to be at her desk at such a late hour. She hurried across and pushed open the door to her father's office enough to peek inside. She let out a quiet chuckle at the notion she was acting like a spy in one of her father's Penny Dreadfuls.

"I wonder what Tyler would think of me, sneaking around like this?" she whispered to the room at large.

"He would think you're up to something that could get us both into a lot of trouble."

Chloe gasped and spun around to find the man that she'd just been thinking about, leaning against the doorframe to the hallway, his arms folded over his chest.

She put a hand over her heart. "You scared the daylights out of me! What are you doing here?"

"I might ask you the same thing. I was stepping off a tram down the street when I noticed someone lurking around outside this building. I got curious and decided to investigate. In case you weren't aware, there's been a few break-ins, and even a couple of fires in the area."

Her heartbeat slowed back to normal. "Yes, I read something about that in the paper." Not sure if she should defend herself or enlist his help, Chloe entered her father's old office to buy some time. She moved to stand next to the bank of long, narrow windows behind the familiar desk. In the gloom, she studied the city's reflection on the wide, placid river below her. Indecision and conflict battled her common sense, as well as her affection for the man who'd followed her into the room. Should she share the information she'd learned in the past forty-eight hours and hope Tyler could offer some advice? Or should she put the man off and deal with the problem herself?

"What would you charge me for some legal advice?" she turned and asked him.

Tyler parked himself on the corner of the desk. "Depends. Do you want to retain my services or is this just friendly conversation?"

Chloe turned back to the window and pulled her bottom lip between her teeth. *Even if I don't fully trust him, the man knows the law.*

He must have sensed her hesitation. His tone became more serious. "What is it, Chloe? Are you in some kind of trouble?"

She heard him move and then felt his hand on her shoulder. "Let me help."

With a tired sigh, she allowed herself to lean back against him. His solid form offered reassurance she hadn't felt in a very long time. "I might be in trouble and I'm not sure what to do about it."

~

As much as he liked the feel of her against him, Tyler stepped back and turned her around. "Talk to me. Maybe I can help, either as a friend or as a lawyer."

She looked up at him. Her eyes dark pools of misery. It was all he could do not to pull her into his arms. He fought the impulse and reached out to run a finger down the line of her jaw. She closed her eyes. With a weary sigh, she moved her face away from his touch. She was so beautiful and so stubborn. "Would it make you feel better if we kept this professional?"

"I think that would be best." She stepped away and sat in her father's chair. A pull of the chain on the green banker's lamp instantly illuminated the desktop and Chloe's troubled face. Tyler remained at the window. What could have her so upset? *Patience, my boy, she'll tell you when she's ready.*

With a sigh of resignation, Chloe started her story. "First, I need you to know that I had nothing to do with what's happening here. Neither did my father. In fact, he's probably pacing the hallways of heaven right about now, trying to figure out a way to come back and set things right."

A sad smile trembled on her lips. "But that's not going to happen, so it's up to me." She sat up straighter in the chair and folded her hands on the desktop. "You see, a few days ago when I gave you the tour, I noticed a few people missing. Key people, who've been here since I was a little girl. After you left, I decided to find out what happened to them. I also took the opportunity to go over the books. I'm not a bookkeeper by any means, but even I could see that things weren't right. Payroll hadn't been paid out in a while, and there was a pile of past due notices and threats of collection. Several of our main suppliers have refused to ship materials until our debt is satisfied.

"Cantrell Firearms has always been a successful business, one with a reputation for quality craftsmanship and honest dealings. Apparently, while I was gone, things changed. Men that were true artisans—who know this business inside and out—were let go. I went to their homes and spoke to them. What I heard made me angry and afraid. Afraid for the company my father poured his life into."

She turned in her seat and looked up at Tyler. "Cantrell's is broke. Thousands of dollars are missing. Orders haven't been filled, and creditors are threatening to sue. Albert Sinclair, our former bookkeeper, noticed discrepancies months ago, but when he brought it to Lucius' attention, Mr. Wheeler said the funds had been *diverted* for a new project.

"Albert watched as more capital was siphoned off, until the company was actually working in the red—something that had never happened before. Albert confided in a couple of the other men, Mike Sweeney and Jack Mitchell, about his suspicions. Together, they confronted Lucius and threatened to talk to me."

The look on Chloe's face darkened.

"Let me guess, Mr. Wheeler told them you were aware of the whole thing and was willingly letting him handle it his way." Tyler had seen the same scenario before—deception, fraud, embezzlement. Someone had their hand in the cookie jar.

Chloe's shoulders and back became rigid. "Yes, he lied to them. I had no clue what was going on until a few days ago. By that time the damage was done, and Lucius dismissed the men who raised the questions."

She stood and pulled her gloves off, throwing them down on the blotter. "I don't know what he's up to or why, but I will do everything in my power to stop Lucius Wheeler from ruining my father's company."

She planted her hands on her hips and turned to face him. The light caught and reflected the facets of a large diamond on her ring finger.

It hadn't been there before. Tyler was sure of that. A mix of emotions came to life and bubbled to the surface. He fought the urge to snatch her hand up and demand an explanation. Instead, he moved from the window and headed across the room to the doorway, where he picked up the coat he'd thrown over a chair. The fact that she'd chosen someone else before giving him a second chance, felt like he'd been sucker punched. He took in and let out a slow breath.

"Chloe, it sounds like you have some serious legal problems. As an attorney, I'd advise you to get a lawyer. As a friend, my advice is to be very careful. Mr. Wheeler sounds like he's worked himself into a corner. From experience, I can tell you a cornered animal will lash out at anything in its way, if it feels threatened."

He could see the confusion on her face at his change of tone. Before she could say or do something to weaken his defenses, he worked his arms into his coat sleeves and settled his hat on his head. With the tip of his cane, he gestured to the ring on her hand. "Maybe you should be consulting your fiancé about all this." He turned, then hesitated. "Oh, by the way, Miss Clare and Abel are both very worried about you. You might want to tell them what's going on. If you decide you need legal representation, you know where my office is."

Before she could answer him, he was out the door.

~

Chloe stared at the empty doorway, then down at the ring on her hand. She'd forgotten it was there. The realization of what he must be thinking made her gasp and run to the door.

"Tyler, please, let me explain."

It was too late. He was gone.

Tears blurring her vision, she stumbled back to the desk where she collapsed in the familiar comfort of her father's chair. "Oh, Daddy, what have I done?"

No answer came.

CHAPTER 32

The third-floor had been his first stop. There he opened and tipped over a dozen cans of stain, solvent, and mineral spirits used in finishing the stocks and handles of various types of guns. The smelly mess spread across the floor, following him out of the door. He took a long pull on his cigar and watched the tip come to life. With the flick of his thumb, he knocked the hot ash off into a pile of shavings. Instantly, a finger of smoke curled up. He smiled.

Back on the landing, it surprised him to find a light on over the stairs. Had he turned it on without thinking? With a dismissive shrug of his shoulders, he crept down the stairs past the second-floor offices and hurried to the row of barrels lined up along the far wall.

Pulling the packet of small candle stubs out of his pocket, he wedged one into the gap where the wooden lid met the edge of each barrel. Once all seven were in position, he lit each one and waited until they showed a nice flame.

Satisfied with his work, he moved quietly down to the first floor and retrieved the two cans of kerosene he'd left there when he entered the building. With quick steps, he maneuvered through the long crates of finished rifles ready for shipment.

He felt a twinge of regret. *It's a shame to destroy a quality made firearm.*

At a smaller stack of crates, he wedged off the top of one and pulled a beautiful revolver from its nest of straw packing. With a satisfied grunt, he pushed it into his waistband and sprinkled kerosene in its place, then splashed the base of the crates as he backed out of the room.

In the gloom, he stopped and relit his cigar with a wood match, then flicked the match toward the puddle of kerosene on the floor. A swoosh of instant flame illuminated the space at floor level and raced over the trail of accelerant.

"Hey, who's there?"

He turned to see a man paused on the landing between the first and second floors. No one was supposed to be in the building! The fire flared up behind him as the wooden crates and straw ignited. It was time to leave.

CHAPTER 33

The shout died on Tyler's lips as flames came to life on the floor below him. The arsonist looked up, then sprinted for the loading bay exit. Small explosions sounded overhead. Gagging black smoke bellowed out of the open third floor doorway.

In the time it took for him to realize what was happening, barrels along the wall to his left began spewing plumes of smoke and flame. *Chloe!*

Tyler turned and raced back up the last flight of stairs as fast as his gimpy leg would allow. Near the top, he missed a step. His bad leg slammed into the edge and folded under him. Pain knifed through his thigh.

"Oh, my gosh, Tyler!"

He looked up to see Chloe standing in the doorway down the hall. Before he could tell her to go back, she ran toward him. She clamored down the stairs and kneeled beside him. Her arm snaked under his. "Let me help you."

Gripping the handrail, he got to his feet. "We've got to get out of here. The whole place is going up."

He grabbed her hand. Together, they rushed down the stairs to the landing. He pulled her back as flames began licking up between the steps. "We won't make it down this way. Is there another exit from this floor?"

Chloe turned. Her skirts gathered up in one hand, she headed back toward the second floor offices. "Follow me. My father had fire escapes installed off the second and third floors last year."

Together, they hurried down the hallway and back into her father's office. Tyler slammed the door behind him and leaned against it. He took in a deep lungful of air. "We don't have much time. This place is a tinderbox."

Chloe ran to the window behind her father's desk. "Help me open this." She strained against the stubborn sash.

"Here, let me do that." Tyler came and put his shoulder against the wood frame. It didn't budge. "That fire escape isn't going to do us much good if we can't get to it."

"Use the chair." She pushed it to him.

"Step back." He heaved it up and swung it toward the window. The impact sent shards of glass raining down to the street below. Tyler broke out the remaining slivers and pulled a drape down to cover the jagged frame. He grabbed Chloe's coat from the floor and held it out for her to put her arms in. "You'll need this."

Smoke crept under the door across the room. Tiny flames grew and scurried along the ceiling, hungry for the supply of oxygen coming in the window. Chloe jumped and gasped as gunshots rang out. It sounded like a battle was going on below them.

"It's just ammunition going off. The casings are exploding because of the heat. Hurry, we don't have much time." He picked her up. She weighed nothing in his arms. There was no time to think about the feel of her so close and what it did to him. He maneuvered her out the window to the steel landing, then eased his bad leg through. He had to tuck his head to his chest to work himself out through the opening.

"Thank goodness Lucius didn't have time to put the bars on he talked about."

"Yeah, that would kind of defeated the purpose of the fire escape."

Tyler leaned out over the rail and looked up. Fire spewed from every window on the third floor like dragon's breath. It was going up fast. Whoever had set the fire had done a good job. The entire building would be engulfed in a matter of minutes. In the distance, they could hear the clank of the city's fire bell sounding the alarm. The building rumbled in protest to its destruction.

"Follow me." He unhooked the ladder and let gravity pull it down. Before it reached its full length, it jammed. Tyler pressed all his strength down against the metal framework. It didn't budge. He looked back through the window they'd just climbed out of. The room was quickly becoming swallowed up in smoke and flame. The ladder was their only chance at escape. "I'll go first so I'll be below you in case you slip, okay?"

Chloe gave him a shaky smile. "Thank you for coming back for me."

"Leaving you wasn't an option." He stepped down a couple of rungs and was at eye level with her. With his thumb, he rubbed at a smudge of soot on her cheek. "Second chances, remember? Now turn around. I'll guide your feet to the rungs. Keep a good handhold until you're ready to move down one."

She followed him down without hesitation. At the last rung, they were still a good eleven feet off the ground. "Okay, you did great, but now I need you to hold on while I jump down then I'll catch you, but wait until I'm ready."

Her answer muffled, Tyler had to assume it was positive. *She's a trooper, that's for sure.*

He extended his full length and came up short by several

feet. The jump was sure to be painful if he didn't manage to land on his good leg. Taking a deep breath and with a big exhale, he let go. His right leg crumpled under him. He threw his weight so that his left side took the brunt of the fall. Tyler clenched his teeth against the instant pain. There was no time to give in to his agony. Favoring his injured leg, he struggled to his feet.

Silhouetted against a backdrop of yellow orange flames, Chloe clung to the steel ladder. An explosion rocked the building—now an inferno lighting up the night sky. The fire escape groaned and pulled against the bolts that secured it to the building.

"Chloe, you have to jump. It's pulling away."

She looked down over her shoulder at him. "I can't. I'm afraid to let go."

Tyler could hear the panic in her voice. He had to do something and quickly, before the whole thing collapsed with her on it.

Lord, give her courage and me strength.

"Work down to the last rung. If you let your legs dangle, I'll be able to grab them. I know you don't have reason to trust me, but you're going to have to, just this once."

~

The air around her filled with hot embers like a snowstorm from the bowels of hell. She could feel the heat of the flames and had a sudden thought of the story of Shadrach, Meshach, and Abednego, and the fiery furnace. They trusted God to save them, and he did.

She looked down at Tyler. His face glowed with the light of the fire. He held his arms up. His eyes pleaded with her. *I need to trust him.*

"Dear God, help me let go," she prayed.

A small cry finished her prayer as she let her fingers relax their hold on the steel bar. The fall was straight out of her nightmares, but instead of her father holding her when she opened her eyes, Tyler smiled down at her.

"I've got you. You're safe now." He hugged her close.

The terror and relief mixed together. She cried into his shoulder.

~

The man watched from the docks a half block away. The fire lit up the night sky. Tiny figures seemed to dance around its base like they were performing some pagan ritual. It would do them no good. The building would be a total loss.

He thought about the man inside. Had he got out in time?

A surge of regret flooded him at the thought of the stranger. No one deserved to die by fire. Not that man, and certainly not his baby sister. The image of her staring down at him, arms outstretched, wretched at his heart.

With shoulders slumped in memory, he walked away.

CHAPTER 34

Chloe stood on the sidewalk amid the rubble and stared at what was left of her father's dream. Part of the walls on two sides had caved in. Blackened lumps of still-smoking machinery dotted the surreal landscape the daylight exposed.

"It looks like a war zone," she whispered.

Clare squeezed her shoulders on one side. Abel gripped her hand on the other. If it weren't for the two of them, she wouldn't have been able to stand upright. Cantrell Firearms had been her second home for as long as she could remember. Now it was gone. Her father's legacy wiped out in a single night.

"Come, child. There's no use standing here feeling miserable. Let's go home and I'll make us a cup of tea and bake up some of those muffins you like so much." Clare tried to turn her. Chloe resisted.

"I need to stay awhile longer." She pulled her eyes away from the smoldering ruins and looked at the concerned face of the woman who'd known her all her life. The Morrisons were all she had left. She fell against the Clare's expansive chest and let herself be cradled in her arms. "Don't ever leave me," she cried.

Clare hugged her close and smoothed a hand down her

back, over and over again. “Ain’t never gonna happen, child. Abel and I ain’t planning on going nowhere lessin’ the Good Lord calls us home.”

Chloe stiffened. The thought of losing them terrified her.

The soothing motion intensified. “Now, now, child. That ain’t agonna happen any time soon. Don’t you worry none.”

Chloe relaxed against her and allowed the familiar motion to calm her tears. Control returned. She pulled out of the black woman’s embrace and rubbed a hand under each eye.

“If it weren’t for you and Abel, I don’t know what I’d do.” She pulled them both to her and hugged them. “You’re all the family I have left.”

“Don’t forget Matthew and John.” Abel reminded her. “They may be out making their mark on the world, but them boys love you like a little sister.”

Chloe allowed herself a small laugh. “They treated me like one, always teasing me about my height and hiding my dolls.” She sighed. “I miss them.”

Abel nodded. “Two years is a long time to be away from family, but Clare and I are proud of them just the same. Last we heard from them, they were doing okay for themselves up there in Alaska. The Klondike Rush is still going strong, but it sounds like they may be getting a little homesick.”

Clare pushed her bottom lip out. “Should be home where I can make sure they get a decent meal once in a while.”

Before the pair could go on about their wayward sons, Chloe stepped back. “Auntie Clare, Abel, go on home now. I’m fine. I need to stay and talk to the fire chief. I’ll be home by lunchtime, I promise.”

“And I’ll see that she keeps her promise.”

Chloe turned to see Tyler standing behind her. Except for the extra support he seemed to need from his cane, he didn’t show any outward signs of last night’s ordeal.

Abel crossed his arms as if he were preparing to do battle. Clare loosened one and tucked her arm under his. "Come on, Abel, after last night I trust Mr. Reynolds will see that Miss Chloe gets home safe." She leaned in and gave the man's arm a squeeze. "Thank you again for saving our girl. She's mighty precious to us."

Chloe smiled and gave the older woman a kiss on the cheek. "And you're both precious to me."

Tyler stood beside her and watched the driver guide the horse away from the curb and head toward the city. Clare waved from the window.

Chloe looked back toward the ruins and watched a few men sift through the rubble. "Does the fire chief know how the fire started yet?"

"I knew last night and informed him before I took you home." Tyler put a hand on her shoulder. "Chloe, it was arson."

Her shock at his announcement gave way to indignation and anger. "But why would anyone do such a terrible thing? We could have been killed!" A new question crowded out the others. "How can you be so sure?"

"Someone definitely set it. I just spoke with the chief." The familiar voice caused Chloe to turn.

Lucius stood behind her. Tyler dropped his hand.

"Lucius, I didn't see you there." Chloe felt pinned between the two men—one her fiancé and the other her rescuer. She looked from one to the other. Both men were giving each other calculated looks.

Tyler finally broke the standoff and extended his hand. "I'm Tyler Reynolds."

Lucius put on a gracious smile and shook hands. At the same time, he reached around Chloe's waist and drew her to him. "I'm Lucius Wheeler, Chloe's fiancé. I'd be interested to know how you came to the conclusion it was arson when the fire chief just now shared his findings."

Chloe tried to pull away. She managed an inch before Lucius' hold tightened. She could feel his tension. "Lucius, Mr. Reynolds saved my life last night. I was in father's office—your office, when the fire broke out."

Lucius' face paled. He looked at her in disbelief. "You were here? In the building? My God, Chloe, you could have been killed!" His concern quickly gave way to suspicion. "What were you doing in my office at night?"

Chloe was at a loss as to what to say. She'd been sneaking around behind Lucius' back for days, gathering information and proof. She intended to confront him, but now was not the time. Before she could come up with an answer, Tyler stepped in.

"I'm Miss Cantrell's attorney. She asked me to meet her last night to discuss some employee issues that concerned her. I'm glad I was there or the man I saw running from the building would have killed her in the fire."

As pale as Lucius had been before, he blanched even more. "You saw the man who did this?" He gestured toward the destruction.

Tyler squared his shoulders. Chloe watched his jaw tighten to a hard line. She'd seen that look before.

"Yes, and I intend to see that he's caught and prosecuted to the full extent of the law. Arson is a felony. Attempted murder could put him behind bars for life."

Chloe looked from Tyler to Lucius. Normally confident and self-assured, Lucius now appeared uncertain and nervous. Why?

Chloe needed time to think. To sift through everything she'd learned and try to make sense of it all. "Lucius, I'm sure you have a million things to take care of right now." She turned to Tyler. "Mr. Reynolds, could you please escort me home?"

Hesitantly, Lucius relinquished her, then grabbed up her hand. "Where's my ring… your ring?"

Chloe looked at her empty finger, shocked and mystified. "I don't know. It must have come off when we were trying to escape."

She kept her face from showing the relief she felt at having the gaudy ring gone. She had intended on giving it back to him, anyway. Now fate had taken that distasteful chore out of her hands, but she still needed to tell him of her decision.

~

Was he mistaken, or did Chloe seem to become more anxious when Wheeler interrupted their conversation? Tyler looked at the man beside her. He had to be a good twelve to fifteen years older than Chloe. Slick and ambitious were words that came to mind. Tyler imagined Wheeler's topcoat probably cost three times as much as the new sack suit he was wearing. He didn't know what kind of salary the man made, but he spent a hefty chunk of it to impress folk.

He thought of the huge ring he'd seen on Chloe's hand and stiffened. If she was looking for this kind of man, he'd misjudged her. Maybe he'd read her all wrong. She talked about second chances and yet turned around and got engaged to a man, who Tyler judged, was probably more interested in her money than her.

It seemed his time and energy were being wasted. Something fragile crack inside him. Focused back on the conversation, he tried to appear disinterested in the lost ring. "I'm sure your insurance will cover the loss along with the rest of the building."

Tyler hailed a passing hansom. "Miss Cantrell, I'm afraid

if I'm going to escort you home, we need to leave now. I have a pending appointment I can't easily postpone."

Chloe gave him a confused look. "Um, yes, of course. I wouldn't want to keep you." She turned to Lucius. "I know we were supposed to attend Suzette Bellmont's dinner party tonight, but I'm really not up to facing a crowd. Could you be a dear and give her my apologies?"

Lucius kissed her cheek and handed her up into the cab. "Of course, my dear."

Tyler could see the man was not happy at the turn of events. He also noticed a patch of bright red skin on his wrist when his sleeve worked up. Was that a fresh burn? From what he already knew—and now this—the implications were too much to ignore.

He looked hard at the man in front of him. Could Lucius Wheeler, Chloe's fiancé, be the arsonist?

CHAPTER 35

Tyler sat in silence. Chloe watched him while pretending to look out the window. What's he thinking? She so wanted to explain about the engagement, but wasn't sure he'd listen or believe her. *No matter what I say, he's probably already made his mind up not to believe me.*

She chewed her lip and searched for the right words. "I think I made a terrible mistake." She shook her head. "No, that's not exactly true."

He folded his arms and looked at her. "What part isn't true?"

"Let me start from the beginning, okay?"

Tyler raised an eyebrow.

"Okay, well first you have to understand my father expected me to marry Lucius."

"He told you that?"

Chloe shrugged. "Well, no, but Lucius said they had several conversations about it. I always felt like Lucius was the son my father always wanted. Anyway, after my father died, and before I left for Colorado, Lucius asked me to marry him. I couldn't give him an answer. I convinced him I was too grief-stricken and needed time." She looked down at her hands. "Honestly, as much as I wanted to find my half-brother,

I was running away from making a decision. When I came back he asked again, and I said yes."

She reached across and laid her hand on Tyler's arm. "You have to understand, that was after you left the house that day, before I knew you were staying in Philly. I didn't think I'd ever see you again."

He adjusted his arm so that it was out of her reach. "So was that the mistake? Should I have gone back to Maryland, or maybe never come out here to see you in the first place? If Lucius Wheeler is the kind of man you want to marry… well…"

"But he's not. I mean, I thought maybe… but over the past few days I've realized he's not who I thought he was." She huffed in exasperation. "Or maybe I only saw the things I wanted or needed to see. I don't know." She shook her head. "The point is when you followed me into that building, I'd already decided to call off the engagement and give him back his ring. I think he cares about me, but there's something he loves more. I thought it was my father's company." She tucked her chin to her chest and played with the buttons on her sleeve.

"I've realized I'm just a means to an end. Lucius' first love will always be Lucius." She lifted her chin. "I almost made the same mistake hundreds of women have made for generations."

Tyler shifted in his seat and threw an arm across the back. "And what mistake might that be?"

"Thinking my only worth was as a wife. That God doesn't really have a special man for me or that I should *expect* to be loved and cherished."

There, she'd poured it all out and left herself open and vulnerable. She went back to playing with her buttons, afraid to look at him. What must he think of her?

Silence filled the compartment.

~

Tyler listened and felt like a heel for making her expose herself like that. He hadn't realized the insecurity she must have felt with her father's death, or the pressure to conform to the role society dictated.

Somewhere in his heart, his spirit soared. She didn't love Wheeler and didn't plan to follow through with the engagement.

He reached across and took her hands in his. She raised her head. Uncertainty and a touch of fear danced across her features and settled in her beautiful brown eyes. She was so vulnerable. And sweet, and stubborn, and everything he'd suddenly realized he wanted in a wife.

He squeezed her fingers. "Chloe, I want you to listen to me and really hear me. I came clear across the country for one reason and one reason only. You. You have dwelt in my thoughts and dreams for months. While I was laid up, I kept remembering your hand on my forehead and you calling me your love."

She gasped. "You heard that?"

Tyler smiled. "So I wasn't dreaming."

The carriage came to a stop in front of Chloe's house. He wished he had more time. "Before you go in, I need to know something. Did you really mean what you said about second chances?"

A smile lit up her face and brought out a dimple in her right cheek Tyler had never noticed before. Probably because he'd never seen her smile so big before.

"That second chance thing works both ways, you know." Her smile faded. "I have to talk to Lucius, to set things straight between us. If you're really serious about being my attorney, I have some information and papers I need to go over with you, especially now that my father's business is gone."

"Just say when and where, and I'll be there. I have something I want to share with you as well."

"I need a little time. The harvest ball is day after tomorrow. Would you be my escort?"

"I'll be here with bells on." The door opened, and Tyler handed her down to the coachman. "And Chloe…"

She stepped to the sidewalk and turned; her face shining with expectation.

"Thank you."

A look of confusion flitted across her face. "I should be thanking you. This is the second time you've saved me." The smile returned in full force. "Thank you, Mr. Reynolds."

Tyler couldn't help the smile that threatened to split his face in two. "My pleasure, Miss Cantrell."

CHAPTER 36

Lucius rang the bell. He stamped his foot with annoyance when it wasn't answered immediately. The fact that Chloe changed her mind about the dinner party should have made him feel better. It didn't. Her tone on the phone was cordial, but lacked any sign of affection. Everything around him was falling apart. After a day spent with the fire investigator, Cantrell's attorney, and the agent for the insurance company, he desperately needed one thing to go right.

The old black man opened the door and gave him a look of indifference. "Miss Chloe is waiting for you in the parlor." He escorted him to the arched doorway. "Miss Chloe, your guest is here. I'll be right outside if you need me." He gave Lucius a meaningful look, as if to put him on notice that he'd be nearby.

Lucius snorted. *Like the old man would ever pose any real threat.*

He turned to Chloe and found her dressed in the same outfit she had on that morning. "Where's your gown?" He pulled out his pocket watch and pressed the lid open. "We're supposed to be there in twenty minutes. You'd better hurry. You know how much I hate to be late."

Chloe moved from the fireplace to the brocade settee.

"Come and sit for a minute, please." She indicated the chair across from her instead of the space next to her.

Lucius got a strange feeling. He took the chair, crossed his legs, and steepled his fingers. She looked nervous but determined. Something was definitely going on and he had a feeling he wasn't going to like it.

"So, are you going to keep me in suspense? You know I don't like surprises."

She looked over at him. Her mouth formed a small 'o' and her eyes widened. "Where did you get that burn on your wrist?"

Lucius pulled his cuff down and rested his hands in his lap. "It's nothing. I was clumsy enough to touch it against a piece of hot metal at the fire site this morning. I'll be okay, but thank you for your concern. Now, please tell me what this is all about?"

Chloe chewed her lip for a second, then raised her chin and set her shoulders. A sign he'd come to know over the last nine years. The muscles in his jaw tensed. "What's going on, Chloe?"

"Lucius, I've come to a decision. One I should have reached long ago. It wasn't until yesterday that I had clarity and I knew I needed to talk to you." Her next words came out in a rush, like she couldn't wait to get them said. "I can't marry you. I'm sorry. If I had your ring, I'd give it back, but unfortunately it's probably gone forever."

Lucius' teeth clenched together so tightly it was a wonder they didn't shatter. This couldn't be happening. It wasn't part of his plan. He let his anger simmer for a moment while he thought of what to say to change her mind.

Her eyes never wavered. "I'm afraid I said yes for all the wrong reasons. I would have made you a terrible wife. We would have both been miserable before long."

She waited for him to say something. He could think of lots of things to say, but what he really wanted to do was shake some sense into her. To convince her she was just a child and didn't know what she wanted. Instead, he played his ace.

"Your father would be very upset by this reckless act of defiance. He expected you to follow his wishes." He feigned a troubled sigh. "I imagine he'd be pretty disappointed in you right now."

Chloe visibly paled. She dropped her eyes to her lap.

Lucius worked hard to hide a smile of satisfaction.

~

The coming confrontation had kept her pacing the floor for most of the day. Even a slice of Auntie Clare's mouth-watering pumpkin pie hadn't tempted her.

"Seems to me you need to be on your knees right about now. The good Lord already has the answers. You just need to ask Him the question." Clare pulled her close. "Child, you're stronger than you know, and smarter, too. That heart of yours knows where you're supposed to be as much as your head does. Your daddy ain't here no more, but God's never gonna leave ya'. That's for sure and for certain. Talk to Him."

Chloe followed her advice and spent the afternoon sitting in her father's chair, reading his Bible. It was when she got up to stretch that the papers fell out and fluttered to the floor at her feet. She picked them up. One was a sealed envelope with Harry written in her father's scrawl across the front. Her lips trembled at seeing the familiar handwriting. He had been thinking of his son? What about her? With nervous fingers, she shifted the bottom paper to the top. Not in an envelope, the single sheet was folded with her name written across one side. Chloe opened it and read the salutation.

My Darling Daughter,

Shaky fingers came up to her lips. She dashed sudden tears from her eyes and sat down, her legs too weak to support her. A couple of blinks cleared her vision enough to read on.

> *Now that you're all grown up, it's time I share my story with you. You may wonder why I never remarried after your mother passed. I was relatively young and successful. The ladies thought I was quite the catch at one time. But my heart could only belong to one.*
>
> *Shortly before I met your mother, I thought I was in love with someone else, but she was married and it pains me to say, I abandoned her when she became pregnant with my child. I'm not proud of what I did and begged God's forgiveness and hers. She accepted my apology, but not my offer of marriage. She returned to her husband. By all accounts, he was a decent man, although hard at times. He never knew about me and raised the baby believing he was his own son. I sent money at the beginning and tried to keep tabs on the boy, but his mother asked me to stop when he was three.*
>
> *I will forever be grateful Anna released me and gave me a second chance at love because I would have never had the wonderful opportunity to meet and marry your mother. You are the daughter of my heart. Your mother was my everything, and I'm so grateful she blessed me with the precious gift of you before she departed*

this earth. My Emily. My Chloe.

You are so like her. Her spirit lives on in you, and I've been blessed to have the honor of raising you and watching you grow into the incredible young woman you are. No matter what anyone may tell you, I want you to know I trust you to follow the future God has planned for you.

I hope you will someday meet your brother and make him a part of your life, as I could not be part of his. He deserves to have the same opportunities my success has afforded you. I have faith that you'll understand and support my wish for him (your brother, Harry) to take over and run Cantrell Firearms, if he has the desire to. You are capable of so much. I don't want my dream to hold you back from achieving yours.

I will assume that since you are reading this, I'm no longer there to advise you. For that, I apologize. It is my deepest wish that you find the love I found with your mother. Treasure it for the precious gift it is because we never know how long we have with those we love.

From heaven's gates and with your mother standing beside me,

Your loving Father

Chloe crushed the letter to her chest. Sobs racked her slight frame, but the tears she shed were ones of joy and release. *He knew!*

She laughed and cried. Clare and Abel found her dancing around the room. Once she calmed down, she shared everything that had been going on, as well as the evidence she'd gathered.

Now they stood right outside in the hallway if she needed their support.

Chloe took a deep breath and stood. She looked at Lucius with confidence. "You're wrong about my father's wishes. I know that now. I also know what you were doing. I don't know why but that doesn't matter." She moved to a side table and lifted a packet of papers. "These are letters—statements actually—that expose you."

Lucius also stood. Chloe could see the trapped look in his eyes. Tyler was right. She needed to be careful of what he might do, yet she couldn't help the anger that boiled up inside.

"I don't understand how you could do this to my father, to taint his memory like this."

"I don't know what you're talking about. Whatever you think you know, you're wrong."

His denial meant nothing. Chloe shrugged her shoulders and turned away. "That will be for the courts to decide. I've already talked to Mr. Stanley. Father's attorney will be by shortly to pick these up along with a copy of the books Albert Sinclair made." She moved toward the doorway. "You have until eight o'clock this evening to turn yourself in."

She could feel Lucius' presence come up behind her. Chloe held her breath. Would he hurt her? She didn't think so, but just in case, Abel stood at the ready, one of her father's pistols in his hands.

"How can you do this to me?"

She turned around. He was seething with indignation. "The better question is how could you do this to my father? A man who loved you like a son. There's one last thing I need to know. Did you set the fire?"

Lucius visibly paled. With a growl, he reached for her. Abel stepped into the archway, the gun leveled at his chest. "I wouldn't do that if I were you. Sir." The last word said with disgust.

"Since Abel has his hands full, I suggest you see yourself out. Good bye, Lucius."

The glass rattled in the door as he slammed out. Chloe let out a long breath. It was over.

CHAPTER 37

He ran a finger under the stiff collar of his new tuxedo and scanned the crowd. Why had she changed the plan and asked him to meet her here? He would have much rather picked Chloe up at her house and escorted her to the ball.

"Relax, my man. The party's just started. She'll be here." Andrew gave Tyler's shoulder a nudge that almost threw him off balance.

"Careful there, Goliath. My face kissing the marble floor isn't the kind of first impression I want to make with these folks. How did you finagle an invitation, anyway?"

"As far as anyone here is concerned, I work in securities, making me legit. It seems Johnny Blue has his fingers in a lot more pies than we originally thought. The investigation into his extra-curricular activities is ongoing. How's your assignment coming along?" he asked in a low voice no one around them could hear.

Tyler fidgeted with his bow tie and scowled. "We have the goods on Wheeler for the Cantrell fire. Police caught him trying to run. He swears he had nothing to do with it."

Andrew huffed. "Don't they all."

"Well, the judge was foolish enough to set bail and somebody sprang him yesterday. I'm afraid he's disappear like the wind. What I'd like to know is who put up his bail money and why."

Tyler didn't want to ruin the evening by talking about Lucius Wheeler. He pulled his pocket watch out to check the time. "She said she'd be here at seven. It's five after."

A giant hand came down on his shoulder. When he looked up, Andrew nodded toward the impressive grand staircase. "Now there's a sight worth waiting for. Wonder who she is?"

Tyler turned to see Chloe at the top of the stairs. She looked radiant in a satin gown of peacock blue. Black lace accented the tapered bodice and emphasized her tiny waist. Long rolls of shiny black curls fell on her bare shoulders. A comb of sparkly blue beads and tiny flowers held the upsweep in place and exposed the exquisite curve of her neck. "Chloe," Tyler whispered in awe. Mesmerized, he stood there until Andrew pushed him forward.

"You're gawking. Close your mouth and get over to the bottom of the stairs before all these other louts beat you to her."

Tyler flashed him a silly grin and made his way through the crowd. The dignified, gray-haired gentleman escorting Chloe stopped halfway down. "Ladies and gentlemen, may I present our birthday girl, Miss Chloe Elizabeth Cantrell."

Applause erupted, followed by a spontaneous chorus of 'Happy Birthday'. Chloe hid a smile behind a black lace fan.

Her birthday? Tyler felt like a heel for not knowing. He hadn't gotten her anything.

~

Two steps from the bottom, Chloe came eye-level with him. "You made it." She eyed his new black suit with its satin lapels, silver gray waistcoat, and bowtie. He was the most handsome man in the room. "You clean up quite well, Mr.

Reynolds."

Tyler smiled and offered his arm. "I could say the same for you, but I won't."

Chloe giggled, remembering what she must have looked like when they first met. Had it really been a short three months ago?

He bent and whispered in her ear. "You, Birthday Girl, are the picture of loveliness."

It took forever to make their way through the crowd of well-wishers. Everyone offered either best wishes or condolences for the loss of her father and the factory. A couple of old biddies made pointed comments on her choice of color for her gown. Chloe smiled and replied, "This shade of blue was my father's favorite. Mine too."

Tyler led her across the room until she was standing in front of the biggest man she'd ever seen. She craned her head back to look up the length of him. At the top, a rugged face grinned down at her.

"Chloe Cantrell, I'd like you to meet Andrew Elliott," Tyler announced.

The giant bowed over her hand. "Miss Cantrell, I believe birthday wishes are in order."

Chloe grinned. "A pleasure to meet you, Mr. Elliott, and thank you. Please call me Chloe."

Her hand lost in his, he patted it. "Only if you call me Andrew."

She looked from the tall man to Tyler. "So, how do you two know each other? Are you a lawyer, Andrew?"

She watched an odd look pass between the two men.

"We both live at Miss Dolly's boarding house," Andrew replied.

Before their conversation could go any farther, Mr. Stanley, her father's attorney, came up to greet them. Chloe made the introductions.

"Mr. Reynolds saved me from the fire."

Mattson Stanley pursed his lips and shook his mane of silver hair. "Terrible business. To think Lucius Wheeler would do such a thing. It's unconscionable. I understand the man has fled the city."

This was the first Chloe had heard of this new development. An uneasy feeling began to churn in her stomach.

Tyler placed his hand on her back. "The authorities are looking for him. Besides being charged with embezzlement and a few other counts, they believe Wheeler's responsible for setting the fire."

Chloe remembered back to the burn she noticed on Lucius' wrist. She couldn't believe he would go so far as to purposely destroy Cantrell's. She shuddered at the thought that she'd ever agreed to marry the man.

"I don't understand what would make him so desperate to do such a terrible thing. Lucius helped my father build Cantrell Firearms."

"Word is, he is quite the gambler, owes thousands of dollars to some pretty rough characters." Mr. Stanley shrugged his shoulders. "Vices can make men do some pretty strange things." He patted Chloe's hand. "The fact that he let the insurance lapse on the building has got to be a hard blow. But don't you worry, dear, I don't believe the creditors will be able to come after you."

His words were meant to be reassuring. Instead, they hit her with a force that took her breath away. "There's no insurance policy? But the equipment, the materials? There were supplies there that hadn't been paid for yet." She felt sick. Bile rose. She pressed a clammy hand against her throat, determined to keep it down. The only clear thought she had was that she needed help.

Oh, God, what am I going to do now? Please help me.

CHAPTER 38

Tyler didn't like how pale she became. He could see the panic in her eyes. He needed to do something quickly. With one arm around her waist, he leaned in and whispered in her ear. "You look like you could use some fresh air." He turned to the others. "Excuses us, gentlemen."

He guided her through the crowd to the tall French doors and out onto the flagstone terrace. Instantly, she began to shiver. He worked his arms out of his jacket and draped it across her exposed shoulders. "Are you okay?"

An anguished sob escaped around the fingers she held to her lips. "What am I going to do?"

Standing behind her, Tyler circled his arms around her and pulled her in against his chest. He bent his head and spoke into the mass of curls that smelled like lilacs. "You're not alone in this, Chloe. I'm right here, and I don't plan on going anywhere."

She turned in his arms and sobbed against his chest. "There's nothing left. I'll never be able to rebuild Papa's company. If I was a man…"

"Shh." His finger under her chin, Tyler tipped her head back. "If you were a man, I wouldn't be standing here holding you like this. If you were a man, I wouldn't have traveled across the country to tell you I love you. If you were a man, I couldn't do this."

He leaned down and let his lips brush hers. "I'm glad you aren't a man."

~

They sat in a circle around the desk in her father's study: Tyler, Albert Sinclair, Mattson Stanley, Mike Sweeney, and Jack Mitchell. They'd spent the afternoon working out the details to see that all the creditors were paid and coming up with a plan to compensate the men until they could find other employment.

"It will leave you with little else but this house, Chloe. Are you sure you want to do this?" Mr. Stanley asked.

Chloe sat up straighter and lifted her chin. "I'm absolutely positive. Cantrell Firearms provided me with a wonderful life. It was part of my father's legacy, but only a part. The important parts were the values he taught me. Loyalty, honor, ethics, fairness, and compassion were just as important to him."

Mattson stood. Everyone else joined him. "Well then, I'll see that everything is taken care of." He reached across the desk to shake her hand. "Oliver would be proud of you."

Abel appeared to escort them all to the door. Only Tyler remained. With the others gone, the room grew quiet except for the crackling of the logs burning in the fireplace.

Tyler came around the desk and gathered Chloe in his arms. It amazed her how familiar and comfortable she felt there.

"I'm proud of you, too," he announced, his chin resting on the top of her head.

She pulled back and looked up at him. "You want to know something funny?"

He smiled down at her, one eyebrow raised. “Sure. What?”

“I feel freer than I ever have. Virtually everything is gone, and yet I’m excited about the future. It’s really true. He’s a God of second chances.”

The End

Dear Reader,

I hope you enjoyed Book 1 of the Wild Justice series. The story came together out of memories I had from time spent at Ann Bassett's cabin in Brown's Park, one of three hideouts the Wild Bunch used. Many of the characters in *Second Chances* were real historic figures; the Bassett family, the storekeeper John Jarvis, the outlaws that frequented Brown's Park, including Butch Cassidy and Sundance Kid.

My father gave me a love for storytelling and was first to share the history of the people that lived around the 'Gates of Lodore' with me. The cabin still stands at the edge of the meadow and the 'blow hole' where Trace met the U.S. Marshalls will be there long after we're all gone.

Tyler and Chloe's new life back east is full of suspenseful moments, historical events, and personal struggles that will bring them back to Colorado in Book II *Fragile Reprieve.* Their struggles continue in Colorado Springs and the gold fields around Victor and Cripple Creek in Book III *Final Justice.*

I hope I wove tales that intrigued and entertained while offering some insight to characters that wandered through the pages of American history.

Until next time, keep your eyes and heart open 'cause you never know what may happen next.

Blessings,

Debra Shelton

Because the digital world of algorithms determines so much of a book's ability to reach audiences, it would be greatly appreciated if you would take the time to provide a review on as many of the following websites as you feel comfortable with.
www.goodread.com
www.bookbud.com
www.amazon.com/Second-Chances-Justice-Debra-Shelton
www.facebook.com/groups/AvidChristFicReaders

Interested in being a beta reader or launch team member for future books or have thoughts to share? Email Debra at sonlightpublishing@gmail.com.

Growing up, Debra discovered books could take her on adventures she only dreamed about. Intrigued by an author's ability to put words on paper to create a scene, elicit an emotion, and encourage imagination, she tried her hand at writing at a young age. A spark ignited and grew into a full-fledged flame when she discovered she could express herself better with written words.

A lifetime later, the adventures she'd only read about became a reality when God called her to Africa. In the bush country of Zambia she went to work building and running an orphanage that became home to an average of eighty-five children. Her experiences and the people she came to know while she was there inspired her first two novels, the *Escaping the Darkness* saga.

Today she is back in beautiful southwestern Colorado, working, writing, and enjoying the opportunity to watch her grandchildren grow and welcoming her first great- grandson.